"Shame Isn't An Emotion I'm Familiar With."

David dragged his hand through his hair. "I've tried to forget you, and found myself watching you instead. I know your schedule. That you're an early riser. And today, when you broke your routine, I was certain something was wrong. I thought—hell, I don't know what I thought. Then I was angry."

"At yourself for caring." Raven's voice was quiet. Once, she'd tried to hate those who made her feel enough to care. She'd been a long time learning that caring again wasn't disloyal to those who were gone.

"Yes." He didn't lie or evade.

"And you kissed me to punish me."

"No, Raven. I kissed you to punish myself."

Dear Reader:

I can't let February go by without wishing you a Happy Valentine's Day! After all, this is the day that celebrates love and lovers . . . and it's very special to those of us at Silhouette Books. What better way to celebrate this most romantic of holidays than with Silhouette Desire?

Our "Valentine's Day Man" is sexy *Man of the Month* Roe Hunter in Laura Leone's sinfully sensuous tale, *The Black Sheep*. Roe is a man you're not likely to ever forget, and he really meets his match in Gingie, one of our most *unique* heroines.

Also in store for you is a delightful romance by Dixie Browning, *Gus and the Nice Lady*. Ms. Browning's love stories are always so romantic, so delightful . . . you won't want to miss this one!

Rounding out February are books by BJ James (her many fans will be pleased!), Anne Cavaliere, Noelle Berry McCue and Audra Adams. Don't miss any of these wonderful books.

And next month . . . Diana Palmer brings us a new miniseries, *Most Wanted,* revolving around a detective agency. The first book, *The Case of the Mesmerizing Boss,* is also March's *Man of the Month*. I know, you won't be able to wait for it . . . but March will be here before you know it.

And until March, happy reading!

Lucia Macro
Senior Editor

BJ JAMES
A STEP AWAY

SILHOUETTE *Desire*

Published by Silhouette Books New York

America's Publisher of Contemporary Romance

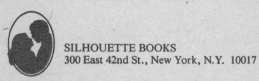

SILHOUETTE BOOKS
300 East 42nd St., New York, N.Y. 10017

A STEP AWAY

ISBN: 0-373-05692-3

First Silhouette Books printing February 1992

All the characters in this book have no existence
outside the imagination of the author and have
no relation whatsoever to anyone bearing the same
name or names. They are not even distantly
inspired by any individual known or unknown
to the author, and all incidents are pure invention.

Books by BJ James

Silhouette Desire

The Sound of Goodbye #332
Twice in a Lifetime #396
Shiloh's Promise #529
Winter Morning #595
Slade's Woman #672
A Step Away #692

BJ JAMES

married her high school sweetheart straight out of college and soon found that books were delightful companions during her lonely nights as a doctor's wife. But she never dreamed she'd be more than a reader, never expected to be one of the blessed, letting her imagination soar, weaving magic of her own.

BJ has twice been honored by the Georgia Romance Writers with their prestigious Maggie Award for Best Short Contemporary Romance. She has also received the *Romantic Times* Critic's Choice Award.

Prologue

"**B**astard. Prissy little..."

Simon McKinzie cut short the next expletive, hunching his massive shoulders against a cloying mist he couldn't escape. Like fog, it followed him, creeping into every cranny of the playground. From the look of the sky over the nation's capital, the worst was yet to come.

Shoving his hands into the pockets of his rumpled raincoat, in damp misery, he watched as Thomas Jeter picked his way through the deserted playground. When he'd chosen the park for this meeting, Simon had envisioned sunlight and laughing children. Safeguards for Jeter's neck. Next time, if, God forbid, there was a next time, he would check with the Weather Service. But now, with hands fisted, his bearlike body as hard as granite, he waited in the dreary June day.

Jeter, an elegant man dressed in sartorial splendor, halted before the big Scot. The mythical protection of a rope swing dangled between them. Setting a designer briefcase on a clump of grass, Jeter stood smirking up at the taller, older man. Like a gentleman farmer planning the castration of a prize bull past his prime, Simon thought. Except this bull wasn't quite ready to put out to pasture with his pride sliced open. Or his throat, or the throats of any of his men.

Jeter rocked back on his heels, using silence as a weapon. Simon looked back. The swing swayed lazily between them. A battle line, drawn by the whim of a summer breeze.

"Simon," Jeter said when the Scot made it clear he would stand all day as voiceless as the mist.

Simon's cold gaze stabbed down at the fashionable attire, the heavy cuff links glowing above the perfect manicure. Distaste burned in his hooded eyes.

Jeter tried again. "Good of you to see me." He gestured at the park. "Only you would think of meeting here."

Simon's lips curled, speaking more of loathing than a thousand words.

Jeter began to fidget. Simon watched him shrug his raincoat to the perfect drape over his jacket and shoot his cuffs the fashionable distance out of his sleeves. Then realizing he'd been intimidated without a word, Jeter forced himself to stop. In an attempt to establish control, he lifted his briefcase and snapped open its clasp. "I have information concerning one of your men."

Simon's gaze flicked idly to the case, then returned with unblinking precision to the bridge of the smaller man's nose. He let Jeter feel the weight of that stare, knowing his reaction was more subdued than expected. As he judged it would, Jeter's confidence bloomed.

Clearly, certain that his listener was hanging on every word, he spoke with perfect diction. "This is of grave concern, Simon. An urgent matter."

"Cut it out, Jeter," Simon said in a deep rumble. "And put your report away. There's nothing you can tell me about any of my men. Especially David Canfield."

Jeter froze. "How did you . . ."

Simon threw back his leonine head, smiling the smile that over the years had sent chills through any who threatened the deep cover of his organization. *His* organization. The special-intelligence organization conceived by a past commander-in-chief, but created by Simon. After fifteen years, it remained so highly secret, it had no recorded name, but among the few who knew of its existence, it had garnered a few. The Black Watch, Simon's Ladies from Hell—both for the strong and savage regiment of Simon's ancestral Scotland.

Members of his elite cadre, in honor of Simon, as well, called themselves simply, The Watch.

"How did I know you'd set your vicious sights on David?" Simon drawled. "Which reason would you like first?" Hand raised, fingers splayed, he ticked off his points. "Reason number one, your hunger for power, a need to control anything and everyone, including Simon McKinzic and his men."

Jeter opened his mouth to deny the accusation, but Simon silenced him with the narrowing of his eyes.

"Reason number two." A second finger folded. "Your fear of anyone who operates beyond your knowledge. You nose into every action, have an ear at every door—" Simon smiled grimly "—but not mine. Sticks in your craw, doesn't it?" Before Jeter could respond a third finger dropped. "Reason number three, you've been looking for a way to bring us down for years. A feather in your political cap to expose a threat to security, guilty or not. Right?''

Simon expected no answer. Finger number four dropped. ''David Canfield is the best of my men and, for the first time, he's in trouble.'' The fifth finger folded. The fist was complete. Simon reached between the ropes, resting his fist's weight beneath Jeter's chin. ''Reason number five,'' he said softly, each word like a silenced bullet. ''You're a vulture. David's the opportunity you've been looking for. You'd destroy him to get to me and The Watch.''

The fist pressed against the prominent cartilage in Jeter's throat. ''Hear me and hear me well. You won't touch David, and you won't use him to bring me down.''

Jeter couldn't stand his ground against the smoldering violence. He stepped back, holding the briefcase as a shield. ''This has nothing to do with you. The man's unstable. The weak link. A coward no one can trust. When his last mission went sour, he left his partner in a jungle.''

''Coward!'' Simon spat. The wet was forgotten, everything was forgotten but Jeter's accusations. God! How he hated these prim little bureaucrats who sat in ivory towers, lily-white hands folded in their laps while better men worked to keep the world intact. ''Listen and listen good. David Canfield did not leave his partner. Not while she was alive!''

''She was wounded and would've slowed him down. We only have his word that he didn't leave her to die.''

''Not we, Jeter, *I*. *I* have his report. *I* shared his grief. *I* have his word. *You* have innuendo.''

"It's fact that he aborted an assignment and came out of the jungle when he could've finished alone. He's operated alone more often than not. Why not again?"

"There were reasons. Extenuating circumstances."

"There are no extenuating circumstances for a man like Canfield. His sort are sociopaths, without conscience. He knows too much. With a few careless words, he can destroy everything we've spent years accomplishing."

"We? Having trouble with your pronouns, Jeter?"

"Simon, you have to listen—"

"No," Simon interrupted, wondering how a biased, cliché-spouting idiot had weaseled his way into the ranks of those trusted with sensitive information. "I don't have to listen. You do. The last thing David is, is a sociopath." Simon wouldn't waste his breath spelling out for a cretin that conscience was one of the key requirements for The Watch and that David Canfield had more conscience than any man alive. Nor would he speak of his own remorse for using that conscience. With an edge of pain beneath the iron, he said, "David's never spoken carelessly. None of my men do."

"They don't resign without warning, either, do they? But Canfield has." A sly smile twisted Jeter's features as he played his ace. "He's a malcontent. Simon, he can hurt you. Hurt The Watch. We have to silence him."

"Silence him? To save The Watch?" Simon's hands gripped the ropes of the swing. "How do *we* silence him?"

"He could have an accident."

"Fatal, of course."

"Of course." Jeter's smile grew smug.

Simon watched it change, thinking the man should never play poker. The idiot considered his point taken, his prey caught. "Tell me one thing, Jeter. When did you decide I'd become a dithering idiot? Was it when you came to the learned conclusion that I'd do anything to save The Watch? Even betray one of my men?"

"No one would know that you—"

"Shut your lying mouth! If I agreed, once the... accident was done, you'd trip over your tongue to leak the truth." The laughter of a single child drifted from a distant hill, but Simon didn't hear it. His whisper was a cold warning of Jeter's mortality. "My men would know I sold David out. You'd see to it."

"No!" Jeter's spurt of confidence was shriveling. "No one will know."

"You're damn right, you son of a whore. Because it won't happen." Simon brushed the swing aside. Stepping closer, he grasped the silk of the smaller man's tie, drawing him onto tiptoes. "Do you know why, Jeter...? No? Then I'll tell you."

"For the love of heaven—"

"Shut up," Simon snarled. "I haven't told you your part in this."

"My part!"

Simon's grip silenced him. "From this moment, David Canfield's welfare will be your greatest concern. Why? It's simple. For your own survival. I have files, Jeter. Proof of every slimy trick you've pulled on your way up the political ladder. If anything happens to David, by accident or natural causes, you'll pay the price."

"You're bluffing. There are no files."

"I don't bluff," Simon said flatly.

Jeter abandoned the pretense of innocence. "There are others involved. Powerful men you wouldn't dare cross."

"Wouldn't I? Is it worth the risk to find out?" Simon hadn't thought that Jeter was in this alone. He was one of a breed, holding no elected office, wanting none. His sort were appointed in payment of political favors and fancied themselves the power behind the government. *They,* not men like David, were the conscienceless, running in packs, with no real loyalty beyond ambition. "Are you willing to give up everything to be the sacrificial lamb?"

Jeter's arguments deflated like a ruptured balloon. He shook his head, "No, I can't."

Simon's smile bared his teeth in a cold rictus. "Then we understand each other. David will be safe as a babe in his mother's arms."

"Yes."

Jeter's sudden capitulation to save his own neck, when only moments ago he was smiling as he planned David Canfield's death, infuriated Simon as nothing else had. "Can you imagine how hard it is not to break your dainty little neck? It would rid the world of one more slug."

Jeter was finally beyond words. He stared at Simon.

"No." Simon granted a reprieve, knowing this change of attitude wouldn't last beyond Jeter's escape from the park. Any who spoke so glibly of betrayal was a stranger to honor. The man was despicable, but Simon had a use for him as David's insurance. "Take this message back to the rest of the slime. Tell them I know who they are. Promise them from me that if anything happens, I'll find them." Eyes as cold as winter bored into Jeter's. "And not one will survive an hour longer than David Canfield.

"Now, go!" He shoved Jeter away, watched as the man clawed at an elusive rope for support, smiled as

Jeter sprawled in the mud. "Get up. Get up and get out. I can't stand the stench of you any longer."

When Jeter was gone, Simon stood listening. Gradually, his anger eased. In his mind, he heard the sound of children laughing, innocent children, one of whom might grow up to be a man like David.

David Canfield. The man who made fact the cliché, "cream of the crop." He was the best of the best. Once, a young idealist with a smile that melted hearts. Not too handsome, too tall, too lean or too fat—nothing striking to draw the eye. The perfect chameleon . . . until he flashed his slow, lady-killer smile. Now, after fifteen years in the field, suppressing honor and gentleness, growing harder and more cynical each day, the smile had disappeared.

Simon shook his head like an angry bull. Sociopath! Just the opposite. David cared too much! It was the caring that made him the best. The caring that had nearly destroyed him. He'd become solemn and cynical. But hard?

"Never," Simon said in the darkening of the imminent storm. An idealist's way of coping. Of surviving. Scar tissue on wounds too awful to face.

He had never denied that he saw what he was doing to his best man. Each time he saw. "And, damn my soul, still I asked him for more." Now David was only a step away from going over the edge. "Or worse." A step away from becoming a rogue, an agent who takes the law into his own hands, wreaking havoc and sometimes death in the name of retribution. David meant to have the traitor who betrayed his mission and caused the death of his partner. The need, coupled with fatigue and remorse that had seethed for years, was driving him to the edge.

Simon sighed grimly, thanking God Jeter hadn't known how close he was to the truth. But, he promised himself, there would be no accidents, no hospitals where doors open only one way and luckless patients disappear. The psychiatrists wouldn't get David, nor the Jeters. Not yet, at least. It was a risk, a dangerous one, but Simon knew he owed David a chance to make peace with his conscience, his work, the world, and to heal himself.

"I know just the place for him to do it." Simon smiled as he added softly, "And the person to help him."

He felt a tug at his leg. A young voice asked, "Who you talking to, mister? Ain't nobody here but you and me. And we're gonna get wet in a minute, we don't go home ourselves."

"I think you're right." Simon knelt before the child who wore only a ragged shirt and faded shorts. "Where's your mother, boy? You shouldn't be in the park alone. You can't be more than six."

"I'm eight, and I'm alone 'cause I ain't got no mother. There's just my granny, and she's always drunk."

A street child, tough, smart, wise beyond his years, like David had been. The sort who fall between the cracks in society. Exploited then abandoned when they were trouble.

"But not David," Simon muttered, struggling with his own conscience. David had been snatched from the streets by the war, and from war by Simon. Now that he was a man with shattered beliefs, he would not be abandoned. "Never David."

"My name's Rico, not David."

Simon's grave expression eased. "Of course, it is." Reaching into his pocket, he fished out a five-dollar bill. "Take this. Buy yourself a decent meal. Don't let your grandmother spend it on liquor."

"No, sir, but maybe I'll buy her something pretty. Make her feel better. Then she won't have to drink to forget the bad stuff." With surprising wisdom, he added, "Can't forget anyway. Trouble's always waitin' when she sobers up."

"She won't forget, but maybe she can deal with it if someone who understands helps her."

"Like me?"

"Like you." Rain that had threatened throughout the afternoon began to fall in earnest. "Looks like we both better run." Turning the child around by his shoulders, Simon patted his head, saying, "Scoot."

He watched until the child faded from sight. His thoughts were of David. Of help and hope. Of a woman whose own life was once in shambles.

"Raven."

The sound of her name brought the illusion of sunlight and laughter and peace to a troubled man standing in the rain. Could she do the same for David?

"Yes."

Simon's decision was made. He would ask David for time. Time for David to make peace with himself and his job. Time for Simon to find the traitor in The Watch.

He turned and splashed to his car. He was going home to make two calls. First, across the city to David Canfield. Second, to the highlands of North Carolina.

To Raven McCandless.

One

―――

David Canfield laid his night glasses aside and leaned back against a boulder. He relaxed, innate caution quieted for a moment. Clouds darkened the moon. He was a shadow blending into the mountain at his back, as much a part of it as the boulder where he sat. The sultry breeze that ruffled his thick brown hair and teased his somber shirt had died completely.

The granite was hard, and he wanted a cigarette. A filthy habit, a dangerous one. One that could buy him a bullet, cheating the medical profession of one more statistic. His smile was grim as he returned his attention to the valley.

An hour had passed since he had settled on this jagged rock overlooking the land below. In the fading light, he'd studied the terrain, the lake and the buildings. There were two cabins, as he had expected, built of weathered wood with bright tin roofs. Both structures were identical, sitting side by side on a tiny hillock beyond the lakeshore. The rise afforded an unimpeded view to the left and to the right. A wall of sheer granite towered at their backs.

The first McKinzies, proud, dour Scots seeking a home, had chosen well. For beauty, for defense. The valley was virtually impregnable—against an expected intruder—with the lake, the mountains and rough granite as its fortifications.

David had come to the valley under friendly duress. The only sort he tolerated, from the only person he'd allowed to exert it. This was Simon's valley, the older cabin had once been Simon's home, and would be David's for three months. He'd promised Simon that much, for The Watch, out of respect.

He'd come, for once doubting Simon's wisdom, and discovered he liked what he saw. From the mountainside, he had committed the valley floor to memory. He knew the number of stepping stones that wound through a wildflower garden and, in the forest beyond, noted a scattering of scarred trees, slashed by the claws of a bear. He found where the eagle nested. Like the eagle, he knew the rise and fall of the land. His gaze had followed the path from the cabins to the lake, losing it for a time beneath the night shade of a drooping hemlock.

He knew the valley like a finely drafted blueprint. It was the woman who was a mystery.

Reaching for his cigarettes, he shook one from the pack and struck a wooden match on the stone. There were no guerillas to smell the smoke or see the flame, yet he shielded its flare with his cupped hands. Drawing smoke into his lungs, he settled back. The match, by habit, he broke and tucked into the pocket of his jeans.

Savoring the smoke, he turned his gaze to the newer cabin and its gardens.

What kind of woman would choose to live in such isolation? Who was she? What was she? Raven McCandless, spinster, friend of Simon McKinzie. Little more than name, rank and serial number...and Simon's good opinion. Spinster. The word evoked the image of a pinch-faced recluse with graying hair pulled into a cruel knot. A misanthrope with shades drawn, hiding from the world.

David rarely presumed. Like the telltale scent of tobacco smoke, presumption could be fatal. But Simon had been oddly reticent. His terse comments—"a special lady, the best kind of survivor"—left David little but presumption.

He smiled into the darkness, listening. The woman he'd presumed a recluse was swimming in the moonlit lake. Presumption shattered. He wondered wryly if the day might come when he preferred the pinch-faced recluse.

Grinding his cigarette out on the sole of his boot, he dropped the butt into his pocket. The last thing he needed was a woman. He wanted quiet and solitude. Perhaps, this night was a godsend. Pinch-faced misanthrope or siren, catching her unprepared would make her ill at ease with him, perhaps alienate her completely. Her disadvantage would be his advantage. Embarrassment and surprise for the lady who swam in the lake would assure his privacy.

Tucking the night glasses into their case, he made one more check of the valley and the lake. His eyes moved slowly, finding nothing amiss in the shadowed land. Quietly, he rose. A soft buzzing sounded from a deadfall behind him. Keeping his body rock still, with the barest move, he turned his head. "I hear you, friend."

Night in the southern Appalachians is not total absence of light. With accustomed sight, David found the rattler coiled and wary. Ancient antagonists, two battle-scarred loners, both too weary to fight. In the gloom, still and unsure, they waited. The beaded tail shivered. David heard the tentative buzz of warning, not anger.

"It's all yours, old fella," he said softly as he inched away. "I'm going to meet a lady."

The path he took was surprisingly easy. Unlike his trek into the valley from the winding, unpaved road, the underbrush was sparse. He was a ghost, gliding easily over rugged ground. Moving from boulder to precipice and down, he worked his way over the rock face with only the moon to guide him. Beyond the harsh wall of stone, on the gentler slope that led to the valley, a little-used trail eased his passage.

He moved quickly, sparing no glance to any of the valley but his destination. With the silent step that had saved his life in the jungle and in civilization, as well, he took up his vigil beneath the concealing cover of the hemlock. The dock that stretched from shore to lake gleamed like a silver track. Glittering water mirrored many bright moons as it lapped at its banks.

He felt the night, its stillness, the quiet. He breathed its fragrance, the scent of honeysuckle and evergreen. The woman who swam laughed, a contented note that drifted over the water like sweet music.

David frowned, disturbed by the sound. It was not the laugh of the woman, he presumed. When she walked from her cabin to the lake, the night glasses told him nothing, revealing only the back of a slender figure swathed in a flowing shirt.

She laughed again, melodic notes so clear, she might have been standing at his side. Something he couldn't identify stirred inside him. Watchful tension loosened for a moment before he gathered it back in. Annoyed with himself and the woman, he took a step nearer the lake.

A menacing rumble, a deep monochord joined by a second, stopped him short. His stare probed the darkness, distinguishing only the shape of stone and willow before the utter blackness of dense laurel. He knew what lay there, watching from the mountain as the huge dogs walked to the lake by the woman's side and took up their watch.

David's attention was riveted on the underbrush. No leaf stirred, no intrusion rustled the thick ground cover. Yet. One ill-advised move, *then* he would be dog meat. But for now, for the second time since coming to the valley, he was being warned away.

"So, now I know how the animal population feels about me." His eyes wandered to the lake as he considered the human element. She would be coming soon. He wondered again what manner of woman she was.

She swam well, barely rippling the lake's surface. The quiet seemed more intense with only the gentle splash of her stroke disturbing it. David could see the bright, ruffled water, but the swimmer was only a dark image. Not even the night glasses would pierce the depths of a lake. He knew little more than he had on the mountain. Only that she was a strong and graceful swimmer, and that her laugh was lovely.

A cloud drifted over the moon; shadows deepened. The bright glitter of the water turned to a lightless black. He could not see her, yet he knew she was near. Then he heard the scrape of her nails on the dock, a cascade of water, the pad of her foot, and in an agile move, she was rising from the dock. For an instant, she stood poised. The still image of her body, lithe, full breasted, lean hipped, burned indelibly in his mind. Spinning slowly toward the lake, she rose on tiptoe, her arms lifted, her body stretching to the sky. Water spilled down her long, black hair and over her naked body, shimmering against her skin like carelessly strewed diamonds. She was a pagan worshiping the moon, a child stretching to grasp the silver globe, a woman paying homage to the night. A mystery.

Swaying, in a fluid move, she swept up her hair. Deftly, she twisted water from it then looped it over her shoulder. Plucking her white shirt, which was draped over a tree limb, she shrugged into it and stood looking out at the lake, listening to sounds only she could hear.

David watched, startled, entranced, his plan to surprise and disturb forgotten. His distraction was shortlived, for on its heels came the shock of unexpected anger. The consuming anger of grief, still too new, too vivid. He'd watched helplessly as a woman who loved life and wanted desperately to live it had died. As he'd held her in his arms, trapped in a war-torn jungle, the life she had treasured had ebbed away. Her death brought home to him how precious life was.

This woman, this Raven McCandless, who lived in sheltered peace, valued her life no more than to risk it for the careless pleasure of a sybarite. Helen Landon had postponed her peace and pleasure to serve The Watch. Now that time would never come for her, and the thankless neither knew nor cared.

Hands clenched in anger, he stepped onto the dock. The woman froze, her hand caught in her hair as she'd tugged it from her shirt. If she felt panic or fear, it didn't show. She was as calm and untroubled as the night.

"Simon didn't tell me Raven McCandless was a fool." David's voice was low, his tone mild. Only the words were harsh. The dogs stirred in the darkness but remained silent. "But then, there was very little he did tell me."

Slowly she let her hair fall to her shoulders. "You're early, Mr. Canfield." Her voice, like her laughter, was lovely. There was no trace of fear or surprise as she added, "You weren't expected until tomorrow."

"I never do what's expected, Miss McCandless. It makes for longevity."

She nodded curtly as if she understood, and David wondered how much she'd been told of him. More, obviously, than he had of her.

"I've been swimming in the lake since I was fourteen, Mr. Canfield." She addressed his first remark without rancor.

"Alone in the moonlight?"

"Alone, and always in moonlight."

"Then you *are* a fool," he said bluntly.

She laughed, the same lyrical note that had drifted over the water. Pivoting on the pad of her foot, she swung about. The last tarrying cloud had swirled from the face of the moon and she was bathed in light as bright as day. "You're very like Simon." Her voice, like her face, was quiet, serene.

She seemed unconcerned that her shirt clung wetly to her body. She made no effort to hide the fullness of her breasts or the hard buds of her nipples. David realized in reluctant admiration that she wouldn't cringe or hide or pluck the transparent shirt from the body he had already seen.

"So are you," he said.

"So am I?" She raised a quizzical eyebrow.

David looked from her body to her face, into her dark gaze. He saw pride, courage and honesty. "Like Simon," he murmured, wondering for the first time if they were lovers. Simon was nearly twice her age, but what did age matter with a rare woman like this?

She stood calmly as he studied her in the light. Simon's special lady. Extraordinary. Exquisite. A woman like none David had ever encountered. Her black hair was swept back from her forehead, not in the puritanical knot he'd imagined, but in a loose, twining rope. Her face was a dusky oval, her features finely drawn. Her mouth made him think of roses. She was not only the most beautiful woman he'd ever seen, there was more, a special quality that reached beyond the surface. There was a serenity in her face and her smile that made men look and look again, wanting to lose themselves in the still darkness of her eyes.

He took a step, drawn to her as if she'd beckoned. The undergrowth rustled. The dogs made no other sound, but David knew he'd been given his last warning.

"Stop. Please," Raven cautioned.

"I know they're there."

Raven's gaze roamed the length of him. He was lean, his shoulders wide, his body muscled, but not heavily. He'd obviously walked in from the main road and down the mountain. No little feat. He'd come a day early to study the lay of the land. Naturally, he knew the valley and its inhabitants. She nodded. Of course, a man who never did what was expected wouldn't be taken by surprise.

"I mean you no harm. Nor them."

"I never thought you did." With a gesture from her, the dogs subsided.

She was a cool one. But neither serenity nor beauty were strangers to stupidity. "You take intolerable risks."

"What risks, Mr. Canfield, and intolerable to whom?" She met his heated look levelly.

David found himself wanting to goad her, to destroy the calm that surrounded her. His gaze moved deliberately over her body, lingering at the thrust of her breasts and at the flat of her stomach. Her body was lush and slender, curved and lean. An invitation.

She endured his blatant survey, still refusing to cringe and hide, refusing the hypocrisy of false shame. Unfounded rage blazed through him. He wanted to shatter the self-confidence that let her stand half-naked before him as coolly as if she were dressed in the finest clothes. Would she be so calm if she was trapped in a mosquito-infested jungle, or as confident if she had to live each day afraid it was her last? Would she be as serene sitting in a pool of blood, waiting for a friend to die?

Would Raven McCandless feel guilty for surviving when others hadn't?

Did it matter what she felt? Did anything matter beyond his promise to avenge Helen? Simon had three months to find the traitor in the ranks of The Watch. David had given his word on it. Three months and he would be free of the pledge and the restrictions of The Watch. Free to find the betrayer, to make him die slowly, as Helen had.

"You risk your life, Miss McCandless, and it's intolerable to *me*."

"Why should what I do with my life matter to you?"

"It matters because I've seen people die who wanted to live. It matters because I lost a friend. A woman who treated life as precious, who never took any unnecessary risks."

"This woman, this friend, she died?"

"Yes." His voice hardened. "She died."

"I'm sorry."

"Don't be." There were worse things than dying. Sometimes, surviving is the hardest. But this pretty woman, living in her pastoral valley, wouldn't understand. She had no concept of torture and anguish. Nor of how, in the end, Helen had begged to die.

"Did you love her?"

David looked down at his hands, remembering the blood, hearing Helen's delirium.

"Mr. Canfield?"

Trapped in his thoughts, he hadn't known she'd approached him. He looked down at her fingers gripping his elbow. Her hand was rough and dry, the nails short. One was broken to the quick. Not the hands of a princess who never left her mountain fortress. Not the hands he expected. Not at all. "No," he said roughly. "I didn't love her."

Raven gave him a puzzled look. There was sadness in his voice, and grief, and something else she didn't understand. "Are you all right?"

"No, *Miss* McCandless, I'm not all right. That's why I'm here. Surely, your good friend, Simon, told you that." Shaking her hand from his arm, he wheeled about and strode from the dock. At its edge, he turned back, one foot on the ground, one on the weathered wood. His insolent stare swept over her. His eyes insulted, his mouth twisted in an unpleasant smile. "I'd appreciate it *Miss* McCandless, if next time we meet, you'd wear some clothes. My head may be a little screwed up, and I've lost a trusted friend, but I'm not blind, and I'm not a monk."

He turned on his heel, angry with the desirable woman she was, but oddly, angrier with himself for his arrogance. He couldn't blame Raven for the life she'd chosen. He had chosen. Helen had chosen. Her choice, in the end, had been fatal.

He stalked to the cabin he knew was his. The moon that had shone so brightly on his skirmish with Raven was darkened by a resurgence of clouds. The path was rough, needing all his concentration. Still, a part of his mind resisted, fascinated, intrigued, refusing to turn from Raven McCandless.

He stopped, straightened and stared at a flickering light. A lamp he couldn't see from the mountain burned cheerfully in a window, welcoming him to his temporary home.

Raven. Was there no escaping her serenity, her loveliness and now, her courtesy? He didn't doubt he would find the cabin cleaned, stocked and ready for him. And he had no doubt whom he should thank.

A part of him not yet hardened by the life he'd lived wanted to turn to her, to repent. Another part, stronger, unrelenting, would not. He resumed his walk, doggedly, following the light left by Raven. At the cabin's steps, he hesitated. Decency struggled to surface again and lost. Shrugging his shoulders against the silent rebuke of his damnable conscience, he climbed the stairs. Resisting the impulse to look back at the lovely woman he knew was watching, he stepped through the door into his dimly lighted sanctuary.

Raven waited until the light was extinguished before she turned away. Another backhanded slap. He'd had no time to familiarize himself with the cabin's interior, and certainly not enough to settle in. The lamp, flipped off immediately, was simply another insult. He was sending her a message, saying, "You did this, and I don't need you."

"Simon, what have you done to me?" she murmured. A chill, common in summer in mountainous altitudes, began to nip at her damp body. Crossing her arms against it, she closed her eyes, shutting from sight the dark cabin that seemed as brooding as the man.

Her life was in order, the valley, a quiet haven. She'd lived here alone for nearly ten years and had never been lonely. Simon first brought her to the valley, and in the end, it was he who had saved her sanity. Over the years, he'd given her much and never asked for anything in return. Now, he was asking, and she couldn't refuse.

"No." She opened her eyes. She *could* refuse. Simon would understand. Turning away, she walked to the water's edge. The valley and the lake were always lovely, but by moonlight, they were breathtaking. They were her peace and tranquility. Looking out at them, she could accept anything, even a stranger who was hard and cynical, who looked at her as if she should apologize for existing. Who ruffled her composure as no one ever had. Who set her heart racing with a roving look and a hurt, bitter smile.

She could refuse. Simon had left her that option.

Yet, she had known she wouldn't from the moment she saw David Canfield, standing like a satyr, lean and hard, dark eyes challenging. Even in darkness, she'd glimpsed the desperate weariness etched on his face, and in his voice, heard the hidden hurt, worn on his sleeve like a broken heart.

He was insulting and arrogant. He would disrupt the tranquil life she loved. And at the moment, he despised her. The next three months could be very difficult, but she wouldn't send David Canfield from the valley. For Simon's sake. For David's. For her own.

She faced the cabin. There was challenge in her own dark eyes as she met the blank stare of the cabin windows. David Canfield was an enigma. Simon had told her little, except that he was a friend as well as a colleague. A special friend who was hurt as she'd once been hurt.

"And bitter, perhaps even dangerous. To himself," she murmured. "But because Simon sent him, never to me."

Tomorrow, when there was no moonlight to play romantic tricks, perhaps she would see him as Simon's friend, no more. Then, if he would let her, she would do what she could. When his three months were ended, he would leave and the valley would be hers again.

The valley had never been lonely before. With the honesty that ruled her life, she knew she couldn't be sure it wouldn't be now. That same honesty would not let her deny the physical tug she felt beneath David Canfield's gaze. He wasn't a monk. His look alone would have told her that if he hadn't. He wanted her, and he hated himself for it.

They were strangers sentenced to a time together. He resented the enforced stay, and she— Raven shrugged. She had no idea what she felt or what she wanted. For the first time in a long while, she didn't understand herself.

Something cold and damp nuzzled at her. She looked down at a Doberman, black as night and as big as a calf. "Robbie. Did you come to see about me?" Kneeling, she wrapped her arms around his sleek neck and rested her head on his. "If I'm acting a little crazy, maybe it's because I am."

Another head, smaller than the first, snuggled beneath her arm. "Kate!" She laughed and tumbled onto the deck with the dogs. "I can't be completely crazy if you love me, can I?"

Like black phantoms, they danced about her, always ready for a game. David Canfield was not forgotten. It would not be that easy. He was simply pushed to the back of her thoughts as she rose to her feet and raced to her own cabin with the dogs in gleeful pursuit.

The sun was lifting over the mountains when Raven woke with a start. She'd slept past her usual time of rising by two hours, and still she was tired. Remembering it was the weekend and her days were her own, she relaxed. Her night had been long and restless, and she'd fallen into an exhausted stupor only an hour before dawn. A week had passed since David Canfield had come to the valley.

Her fears that he would disrupt her life were unfounded. On his first day, he walked out of the valley, bringing back his car and belongings. Then he virtually disappeared. There were signs of life in the cabin, a light here, another there, but no evidence of David. Raven settled into her own routine, working among her flowers in the morning, then driving over the mountain to Madison, to the college where she taught. Her evenings

were spent on the illustrations for a book on wildflowers she'd written. When she was tired or restless, she
relaxed at her potter's table.

She had convinced herself she'd put the interloper
from her mind. Then, for an unfathomed reason, her
thoughts were filled with David Canfield and his trouble. She thought of the woman who treated life as if it
were precious, who never took an unnecessary risk. The
woman he did not love. Somehow, Raven knew her
death was the source of his pain.

Perceptions of death and loss dredged up old grief,
and she'd spent the remainder of the night sweating and
shivering, her eyes dry and burning. She hadn't cried
since she was fourteen. Sometimes, she wondered if all
the tears meant for a lifetime had been shed then.

Denied their release, she'd tossed fitfully in her solitary bed. Grief was finally exhausting and sleep, mer-
cifully dreamless. In morning light, sorrows of the
darkest hour were eased. The lost would always live in
her heart, yet she'd learned to go on and not to hate—
to see beauty about her and believe the world was good.

Simon taught her it was an insult to those she'd lost
to destroy her life with grief. She fought him, determined to punish herself for living. Then, gradually, she
understood. Life ends, but so must grief, and the end of
grief is serenity. Raven lived her life by this rule and only
rarely forgot. Last night was the first time in a long,
long while.

"But it's done now, and I'm stronger today than I
was yesterday because of it."

Rising, she went to the bath to splash cold water on
her face. Her next stop was the kitchen to make coffee.
While it perked, she dressed for her run with the dogs.

They would be waiting for her, sprawled before the door where they spent every night.

Tossing her sleep shirt aside, she drew on sweats, a T-shirt and worn, comfortable running shoes. Her hair was braided, requiring no attention. All that was left was collecting Robbie and Kate. She ran five miles with the dogs each morning. Running swept away the cobwebs of sleep and left her eager for the day.

She was out the door and down the steps with the dogs at her heels when she realized David was walking by the shore. She stopped short, surprised and disconcerted. He seemed contented with his solitude. With only a wave of acknowledgement, she headed in the opposite direction. She ran hard, her long legs stretching out in a ground-eating pace, exorcising disturbing thoughts of David from her mind.

Robbie caught her mood and picked up his pace, racing ahead faster and faster. Raven suspended all thought and ran for the sheer pleasure of running. When they made their turn and headed back, dodging over the worn trail, she picked up the pace even more.

The path David had taken was deserted. She felt a flutter of distress. His troubles would only intensify if he shut himself away to brood. As she approached her own cabin, she saw he was sitting on its steps.

Winded and dripping with sweat, she stopped before him. Her heart was too full and her breath too short to speak. Resting with her hands on her knees, she wondered if the man planned to make a career of catching her at inopportune times. When she could straighten, she found herself looking into his solemn face.

"Are you all right?" He didn't touch her, but something in his expression said he wanted to.

Raven shrugged and managed a nod. Gradually, her panting slowed. "Why do you ask?"

"You were late. Then you ran as if demons were chasing you. I thought . . ." He shrugged.

He hadn't shut himself away as completely as she supposed. He was aware of her schedule. Raven was surprised. Concern had drawn him from his shell. Gathering her thoughts, she tried to reassure him. "I had a late night and overslept. There's nothing wrong, really, but thank you for—"

"Then you really are trying to kill yourself, aren't you?" He cut her off. The hard edges of his face had grown harder, the lines about his mouth deeper. His somber look became cold, angry censure.

"I beg your pardon?" She was startled by the change and puzzled by his accusation.

"Anyone who runs through the woods at the reckless pace you do is asking for a broken neck. Any fool who runs so hard at the end of a distance run is courting a heart attack. *If* she survives the woods."

Raven stifled a gasp. David's eyes moved with a look of satisfaction to the thrust of her breasts against her shirt. She ignored the look. If this was mere concern, his anger must be something to behold. He was goading her, spoiling for a fight. With as much dignity as she could manage she stood her ground, making a bid for peace. "I've been running the woods as long as I've been swimming the lake. And just as fortunately."

His look ranged over her, much as at the dock. His eyes touched on her disheveled hair, her flushed face. The sherry gaze traced the tilted line of her breast beneath the sweat-soaked T-shirt, lingered as it had before, then returned with painful deliberation to her face.

"Thank God, at least you don't run without your clothes."

Don't, Raven warned herself, for his anger was an expression of anguish. Solemnly, she quipped, "I've been tempted, Mr. Canfield, but I'm deathly afraid of chiggers."

A reluctant grin tugged at his lips, then he laughed, a hearty, deep-throated laugh. "So am I, Miss Mc-Candless. The little monsters leave a powerful itch."

Raven's laugh ebbed to a smile as she offered her hand. "Shall we let our mutual fear be the basis for a truce? This valley was never meant to be a war zone, Mr. Canfield."

He rose from the step. There was no insolence in the look that searched her face. After a moment, he took her outstretched hand in his. "My name is David."

"And I'm Raven." In sunlight, she saw his hair was deep brown, not black. He'd appeared taller, broader, towering over her on the dock, but he was a bit under six feet. With his anger disarmed, there was still lines bracketing his mouth and furrowing his brow. His days shut away in the cabin hadn't been restful. He was exhausted, and had been for a long time. Her tender heart forgot his hostility. "There's fresh coffee in the kitchen if you'd like some."

"No." He hesitated, then flashed a smile that startled Raven anew. "Yes! I'd love coffee that doesn't taste like black shoe polish."

"Yours?"

"How did you guess?"

"Deduction. Strong men like strong brew."

"Not that strong."

Raven smiled. "Then come in and sample mine."

Two

David sprawled in a chair in Raven's sunny kitchen, watching as she took earthenware cups from a cupboard. There was an economy of effort in her moves. Then he realized she was simply skillful with her hands. She pulled a pan of cinnamon rolls from their wrapper. Homemade, once upon a time, she said. Now fodder for the microwave. As the scent of spice swept over him, he knew it was delicious fodder.

Raven set the rolls on the table and sat in silence as David ate. When he picked up the fifth roll, she laughed. "You were starving!"

"I was working yesterday. Hunger keeps the mind sharper."

Raven wondered how many times, in how many places, he'd only had his hungry mind to depend on.

David looked into a cup marked by a dogwood blossom. "How much do you know? What has Simon told you?"

"That you work with him. Secret and dangerous work that he never speaks of. Specifically of you, only that you're tired and troubled, in need of rest."

"Little enough, but more than Simon told me of you."

"There's little to tell."

He gave her a long look, and then he smiled. "I doubt that, Raven McCandless."

His smile was nice, but Raven was wary of their truce. She watched him over the rim of her cup.

"How did you meet Simon?" David asked abruptly.

"It's a long story. Too long."

"One you don't want to tell." He pushed back his chair and walked to the door of the terrace overlooking the valley. "Then tell me about the cabins."

"The original was built by the first McKinzies to come to the Carolinas nearly two hundred years ago. After it burned, the cabin that exists today was built on the site. I spent some time there with the McKinzies. After I finished college, I came back."

"And built your own cabin."

"Yes." Raven moved to his side. "The McKinzies scattered for one reason or another. Only Simon returns. His mother, Rhea, came here as a bride from Scotland, and he was born here. He loves the valley."

"That explains his occasional burr, and yours."

"The Scottish roll of the *R*. You have a good ear."

"When Simon comes, are you lovers?"

Raven went very still. Her eyes were glittering when she looked at David. "I love Simon, and I owe him more than I can ever repay, but we aren't lovers, Mr. Canfield.''

"Then he won't mind if I do this." David caught her braid in his hand, wrapping it about his palm, drawing her gently yet firmly to him. Something seethed in his eyes as his mouth closed over hers.

The kiss began like a punishment. The crush of his hand held the promises of bruises tomorrow. The thrust of his body was harsh and unyielding, but Raven stood pliantly, refusing to fight. Slipping the band from her braid with his fingers, he stroked the tangles from her hair. Murmuring something low and unintelligible, he drew her closer.

Raven's head was muddled, her heart racing. She was confused by the anger in him, bewildered by his tenderness. His kiss deepened, softened, tasting of cinnamon. She had never been held as he was holding her nor kissed as he was kissing her. No man had ever disturbed or provoked or intoxicated her as David.

As abruptly as he'd taken her in his arms, he released her. With his face close to hers, his hand still tangled in her hair, he murmured, "Did you know how much I wanted to do that the first night? The night I met the lovely, elusive Raven. I've watched you running over the mountain, with your cute little T-shirts plastered to you like a second skin. I've seen the way you move, confident, self-contained, as if there was no one else in the world.

"How many men have you driven mad? How many have you teased with your lush body and cool ways? Fire and ice. The cliché must have been intended for you. Were you born like Lilith, with the knowledge to tempt men? Or have you learned from experience that an untouchable woman is a dare?"

He ran a knuckle down her cheek and neck to the round top of her shirt. "No man walks away from a dare when it's as beautiful as you." The tip of his finger rested at the hollow of her throat before dipping beneath her shirt to the cleft between her breasts. Before she could shake off her inertia to protest, he said softly, "Be careful with your dare, pretty Lilith. You might run into a bad guy like me, who doesn't know the rules of your smug little world, who might not play by your rules."

"Mr. Canfield . . ."

"Shh." His finger retraced its path, stopping this time at her lips, stroking them with a light touch. A reminder of his kiss. "I'll see you later. Have a good day." He walked to the door with the step of a man accustomed to moving quietly and quickly. With the valley at his back, he paused. His eyes met hers, keeping them.

"My name is David," he said, and then he was gone.

"Have a good day! Sure," Raven muttered, ripping up a weed with particular relish. The dogs, lying in the shade with their noses buried between their paws, lifted their heads curiously. Raven didn't notice, and in a moment, they returned to snuffling in the dust.

"Fire and ice? Who? A matter of opinion." Plucking the last drooping passion flower from its vine, she glared at it accusingly. The irony of its name escaped her. "Lilith, indeed."

Shifting gingerly, she rocked back, folding her legs beneath her until her weight left her aching knees. Looking along the garden rows boasting of neither grass nor weeds, she was astonished at how much she'd done. In the fever of unrequited temper, she'd done two morning's work in one. Brushing the hair that had escaped her braid from her face, she acknowledged the pristine condition of the garden for what it was—proof that her temper was not completely unrequited.

At least it was the garden that reaped the benefit of her rare loss of control. David Canfield hadn't had the smug satisfaction of witnessing a three-alarm spectacle, and her whirlwind invasion of the flowers had put his taunts in their proper perspective. Now, looking down at her favorite gardening shirt, faded and worn, and at jeans that had seen better days, she could laugh. "Lilith? Ha!"

She decided there was nothing like good, hard labor and unladylike sweat to improve one's mood. And she was definitely in a better mood. Pleased with herself and smiling, she started to rise and stopped. Suddenly, as much from the prickling at the back of her neck as from Robbie's perking ears, she knew that David was close. Her breath grew shallow. Her pulse throbbed in her ears. Every sense was heightened, remembering the strength of his arms about her, the desperate hunger in his kiss. The scent of wildflowers, sweet and heady, became the taste of cinnamon.

Kneeling there in the dust, with the sun burning down, she felt the rising flush of heat that had nothing to do with sun or with anger. The trill of sexual attraction, the man-woman awareness, was new to her. She wanted to deny it, but she was too much the realist to fool herself and too honest to try.

She'd been drawn to this stranger, who'd walked out of the darkness with cruel words on his lips and pain in his eyes. He mystified and tantalized her. His challenging stare rocked her to the core, threatening everything she believed of herself. For whatever reason—because he was a man who had been without a woman too long;

because he simply needed a woman, any woman; or because Raven McCandless excited him—he wanted her. It was in every look, every gesture, every harsh word. He wanted her, and it was tearing him apart.

He had kissed her. A kiss begun in anger, leaving no part of her unscathed. A kiss oddly tender beneath the anger. When he stepped away, she found she needed more. That need, not David's brooding hostility, nor his bitter arrogance, was the source of her malaise.

"And what do I do about it?" she asked as she smoothed the soil about a flower for the third time. Busy work, solving nothing, she knew as she forced herself to stop.

The valley was her home, she would not leave it. It seemed imperative, for many reasons, that David remain in the valley. He'd given his word he'd stay. They were locked into an intolerable situation that neither could change. Raven's only recourse was to make the best of it. She must ignore his resentment, hold her temper and conquer what was probably a naive fascination with a sophisticated man of the world.

Control. No matter what he said or did, that was the key to peace. Control, she repeated to herself in grim silence as, with a lift of her head, her gaze collided with David's.

He didn't acknowledge her. He simply stopped where he walked by the garden's edge. His lean body was taut, his golden brown gaze brooding. Raven smiled at him, a smile meant to reconcile. David's look traced the line of her mouth with a lazy, intimate knowledge. Raven's smile faltered; her lips began to throb with the memory of his kiss. As if he could read her mind and was pleased by her discomfort, he smiled. It was only a subtle quirk of his lips, but she knew exactly what it meant.

He was goading her again, taunting her with his silence and his smile. He wanted to anger her, to splinter her composure. If she were male, he would pick a fight, going toe to toe, spending his rage. Then bloody and battered, happy as a clam, he would step up to the nearest bar and drink himself silly in celebration.

He was out of her league, but she would much prefer the toe-to-toe battle to this war of silent staring. Why should he stay when the valley was so abhorrent? No, she corrected, when *she* was so abhorrent. Simon would release him from his word if she explained how intolerable this was.

Intolerable for both of them. If he wanted a fight, then he would have it and control be damned. Raven tossed her newest resolution aside without a qualm. He was spoiling the valley with his antipathy, and he wouldn't go unchallenged. Anger, rare and white-hot seared her.

Her head snapped back, her gloves were stripped off and thrown like a gauntlet. Her knees hurt. Her shoulders were stiff. Her mind was one dark pain. She hadn't asked for this, any of it. The valley was more than mountains and water. Before David came, it was peace and security and, most of all, the absence of grief. It was her valley. Hers! He would not destroy it.

Anger serves thee not. Rhea McKinzie's voice murmured from the past.

Perhaps not often, Rhea, but this time, it will, Raven answered in her heart.

Before she could rise to charge into the battle she wanted, needed, he was crouching down to her. On his knees in the dirt, with his face only a little above her own, his hands cradled her head, his thumb stroked her cheek. Raven struggled to keep her anger, searched for the words of fury and found they were forgotten.

His eyes strayed to her mouth, lingered. His gentleness disconcerted her. He was as inscrutable as stone, kneeling in the dirt, holding her as if he'd discovered a mysterious treasure. His thumb ceased its stroking and moved over her temple to her forehead. His fingertips trailed down her cheek and jaw, tarrying at the base of her throat.

"What am I going to do with you?" he asked softly. "I came to the valley full of hate, with a burning need for revenge. I didn't want to feel. I didn't want anything or anyone. I'd given my word to Simon that I would put my troubles aside for these three months. I would come to his beloved mountains, I would rest and recuperate, but nothing would divert me."

Snapping a daisy from its stalk, he tucked it in her hair. His gaze was on the flower, concentrating on it. "I hadn't reckoned on Raven McCandless. Proud, strong, beautiful Raven, who beat me at my own game. I invaded your world and found you naked and wet from a swim. I wanted to shame you, yet you never flinched, never gave me that satisfaction. Perhaps the victory's yours, for you were driving me out of my mind. When I was cooler, I realized what I'd done, that I was the intruder in your valley, and I was ashamed.

"Shame isn't an emotion I'm familiar with or that I like. I tried to forget you, and found myself watching you, instead. I knew your schedule. That you're an early riser. Today when you broke your routine, I was certain something was wrong. I told myself you weren't my concern, that I didn't care. All the convincing in the world didn't work. Not even a walk by the lake. I had to know why you were late. I was coming to you when you came running down the trail as if the devil himself were after you. I thought—'' he dragged a hand through his hair ''—hell, I don't know what I thought. Then I was angry.''

''At yourself for caring.'' Raven's voice was quiet. Once, she'd tried to hate those who made her feel enough to care. She was a long time learning that caring again wasn't disloyal to those who were gone.

''Yes.'' He didn't lie or evade. Somehow, Raven knew he never would.

''You kissed me to punish me.''

''No, I kissed you to punish myself.''

Raven nodded. She understood that, too. Compassion stronger than any anger constricted her throat. With her hand, she cupped his cheek. ''David.''

''Don't!'' His grip was like a vise, dragging her hand away. ''You don't know the kind of man you're dealing with. I'm only half-civilized. I've seen things and done things...'' He loosened his grip, but kept her hand in his. ''I've never dealt with a woman like you.'' Not a woman who looked at him as if she knew his grief and regret, as if she wanted to hold him and ease his anguish. Pity he could fight, but compassion unnerved him. ''I don't understand you. I don't want to.

''Stay out of my way. I've apologized one time, and apologies don't come easy for an arrogant bastard like me. So stay out of my way. If you don't—'' his gaze settled on her mouth hungrily ''—if you don't,'' he continued hoarsely, ''I won't apologize a second time.''

''All right,'' Raven agreed mildly, not bothering to point out that he had come to her, that his apology was one she hadn't wanted. Oh, he was arrogant, all right, and calling him half-civilized might be stretching the point, but he was a good man.

She stood, looking down at him. "I don't know what burr you have under your saddle, but I know you've lost someone and I'm sorry." She stopped, crossing her arms over her breasts in an obdurate gesture. "There, that's not quite an apology, but it's as close as I'm going to come. Apologies come hard for naive, little provincials, too. So there won't be another." As if the digression hadn't occurred, she continued. "Losing hurts. This woman who loved life, maybe you weren't in love with her, but you cared for her. As a friend, a colleague, someone you respected." Raven hesitated, then played a hunch. "There's more to this. Your trouble isn't just the loss of a friend."

"Simon didn't tell me you were a shrink. Where do you hang your shingle?"

"It doesn't take a shrink. Living is more than existing. For some of us, it's sadness, and we become so familiar with it, we learn to see it in others."

"What would you know about living, locked away in a paradise where nothing ever touches you?"

You touched me, David Canfield, she thought.

"Is that why you leave the valley every day, Raven? Is there someone who touches you? Who makes you feel you're a part of the real world? Do you descend into the filth for a while, then come back to this?"

He was taunting her again, trying to drive her away with sarcasm. "Who are you trying to convince that you're a terrible person? Yourself? Me? If it's me, forget it. Heaven knows why, but Simon thinks you're worth salvaging. He sees something in you that you don't see, and at the moment, neither do I. But it's there. I have to believe it is, for Simon's never wrong."

"Simon's nearly twice your age."

"Don't!" She leveled a finger at him. "Don't you dare tarnish what I feel for Simon with your ugly insinuation."

"Then tell me what he is to you."

"The same as to you. A friend who saw something in me worth salvaging." She turned on her heel and without looking back, left him crouching in the dust. The dogs looked curiously from Raven to David before they followed her to her cabin.

David's anger vanished like summer smoke. He felt an irresistible urge to laugh. Not at Raven. At himself. She'd taken his arrogance and turned it back on him. She'd accepted his bitterness as natural, something to be endured, a thing that would pass. She'd been impervious to his insults—until they maligned something she held inviolate. Then she marched away, back straight, eyes flashing, leaving him crouched in the dust like a scolded boy. The thought of being bested by such an innocent drew a silent laugh.

"Hey, sweetheart," he yelled between stifled chuckles. "Your face is dirty."

A hitch developed in Raven's step, a little stutter in her feet. Then she stopped, fists folded at her side, back straight. One deep breath shuddered through her, then a second as she said without turning, "Thank you."

"And she marched up the steps and right out of my life." David had no idea he'd spoken aloud. Lifting a frosted bottle, he drained the last of the beer in three swallows. Leaning back in his chair, with his feet propped on the table before him, he squinted at the label on the dark bottle. "Hell, a man can't even get drunk without a woman." Raven had bought the beer, stocking the cabin with his favorite brand, compliments of Simon.

He wasn't drunk yet. Deep down inside, he knew he wouldn't be. The part of him that had spent too many years protecting his back wouldn't let him. "Even in paradise, I can't relent. Paradise." He shrugged and scowled, then tossed the bottle into the can by his chair, listening as it shattered over its predecessors. He considered going for another and decided it was pointless. Too many careful years.

From the floor, he gathered a sheaf of papers. He'd studied them for hours, checking the log of briefings against the traffic in the offices of The Watch. Who was in? Who was out? Who could've breached Simon's legendary security? The answer was always the same. No one. Only he and Helen and Simon were present the day the ill-fated mission was planned. The rest of Simon's people were scattered over the world on assignments.

"Who knew? And how?" Before coming to the valley, he'd studied the papers until he knew them from memory, and the answer was always the same. No one. Yet there had to be something in these records, something he was missing. Tomorrow, he'd call Simon to ask for other files. Perhaps they would hold the answer, and perhaps then he could concentrate.

He flung the papers aside. "Who do I think I'm kidding?" Sure he knew exactly what was in the papers, but he had gleaned little from them lately. For three days, since he invited her to stay out of his way, he'd thought of nothing but Raven.

Following the confrontation in her garden, Saturday had passed quickly as he busied himself with the chores a solitary man must do to exist. On Sunday, he copped a book from Simon's collection on law, reading only long enough to remember why he hadn't gone into law. For the rest of the day, he prowled the house and later, the trails. Once, he glimpsed Raven running, with Robbie and Kate dancing at her heels. On Monday, her routine began again and she left the valley, driving a four-wheel-drive vehicle with an exotic name that looked as if a hard breath would blow it off the mountain.

David, who'd spent the majority of his life alone, was inexplicably lonely.

Today was no better. The valley was filled with a hollow silence. As he had every day, he worked and studied, learning nothing, absorbing less. Then, desperate to put her out of his mind, he ran, blazing new trails over the valley floor and scaling the mountainside. Thorns tore at his clothing, leaves caught in his hair, a scattering stone bruised his ankle. He was a demon, ranging the land, unfeeling, uncaring, driving himself to exhaustion. When he stumbled back to the cabin, he was soaked with sweat, every muscle ached and his mind was at ease.

He'd worked then, managing to accomplish more than before. In telephone logs recording incoming and outgoing calls at the office of The Watch, he found one from Helen's desk to a strange number. A date? A doctor's appointment? David shrugged. It could've been anything, even a call made by someone else using her phone. Except, when he double checked the date, he found no one was in the office but Simon and Helen and himself. So she had definitely broken the rules and made a personal call. Not exactly a smart move, but it had been done before.

He had been making a note to have the number traced when Raven's ridiculous little car had clattered into the valley and it began all over again.

She'd hurried into her cabin, a bag of groceries in her arms. Next, she was in the garden, a basket over her arm, a pair of shears in her hand. She hadn't changed, and as she strolled the rows of flowers, she bore little resemblance to the woman he remembered grubbing in the dirt. In her slim, snug skirt and softly ruffled blouse, she was cool perfection, but strangely not ill-matched with the wild profusion of her garden. As he walked to the cooler to get his first beer, he'd wondered how many people Raven McCandless was.

From that point, the evening went downhill. He found himself lurking near the windows like a voyeur, catching glimpses as she loped across a meadow with Robbie and Kate, and brought a sheaf of papers from her car. Once, when she hauled a heavy box from the trunk and lugged it across the yard, he was tempted to offer his help. But with a particularly caustic expletive, he remembered he was the one who insisted they co-exist separately. So he watched, feeling like a jerk as she struggled up the stairs and out of sight.

All right. Fine. It was nearly dark, she would stay in for the night. Out of sight, out of mind. The cliché was a joke and he knew it, but he'd settled down with one of Simon's books, this time a novel. He'd read the same page twice when he heard the soft slam of her door. The moon was full, and he hadn't a doubt where she was going.

She would wear a swimsuit in deference to his presence in the valley. "And look damn good," he had muttered, opening the second beer and the third, and then lost count. None had erased the image of her as he'd first seen her: lost in a rippling pool of mirrored moons; laughing like a child in secret delight; rising on the dock like Aphrodite, with her body silvered and shimmering with water. Breasts swaying gently with each move. Her waist curving delicately into the flare of her narrow hips. The fall of her dark hair as she rose, arms outstretched, worshiping the night like a pagan.

He sat, unable to work for every detail, every nuance and line was etched into his mind. "Everything," he muttered as he went for another beer after all, giving the label a baleful look, reminded of Raven's kindness.

Raven! Everywhere he turned, it was Raven. Lifting the bottle in a toast to the source of his misery, he gulped its contents down in one try. "In this, the year of our Lord, nineteen . . ." He couldn't remember the year, and knew he was farther gone than he thought. "In this, the year of our Lord, nineteen whatever, David Canfield, spy *extraordinaire,* lost his mind."

He chuckled at his foolishness and was sober enough to wonder if tomorrow, when the hangover hit, would he still think it was funny. The retribution that awaited him sent him into a second fit of laughter.

A sound cleaved through his laughter. He cocked his head as if trying to identify it, but he knew it was the sound he'd been waiting for, Raven's door closing quietly. Her swim was done. She was back, safe within the walls of her home.

David didn't realize until that moment how anxious he'd been. She was maddening and enchanting, and it worried the hell out of him that she swam alone in a lake that was cold on the hottest of days. It was absurd to worry. By her own admission, she'd been swimming in the lake alone at night long before he arrived. When he was gone, she would swim.

"So quit your worrying, fool." Before the words were out of his mouth, he knew he couldn't. Perhaps it was his punishment for coming into her valley like a raiding cossack, trampling over the tranquil life she'd made for herself. Maybe the loneliness he felt was the price he must pay for slapping a hand that had offered only friendship.

"That can be remedied." Then, "Of course, it can." Tossing the bottle aside, he made his decision. He brushed away the stench of beer and splashed water on his face. When his hair was carefully combed, he selected a fresh shirt and slid into it. No sense looking and reeking like a tramp when he wanted to make peace with a lady.

Before he could have second thoughts, he was out the door, down the steps and halfway across the adjoining yards. At her first step, he hesitated. It wouldn't work. She hated him. If she didn't, she should. His gaze fell on the rows of flowers, their colors muted, made more striking in the moonlight. They would be his peace offering.

When he knocked on her door, he carried a randomly chosen bouquet of Raven's own flowers. The door opened, slowly. He braced himself. It would serve him right if she slammed it in his face.

Instead, she stood framed by the light at her back, hands on her hips. She had dressed in a loose caftan, one of the one-size-fits-all sort. If camouflage had been her intent, the soft, clinging fabric defeated her.

"David," she said after an interminable time. "Are you going to come in, or do you prefer standing there all night?"

"I was afraid you might slam the door in my face."

"I was considering it."

"But you didn't." Her hair was still damp from her swim. Memories flooded his mind.

"No, I didn't." She smiled at him and moved aside.

David stepped past her and was assailed by the scent of baking bread.

"I suppose those are for me." Raven gestured to the haphazard bouquet.

"A peace offering."

"I see." She studied him solemnly, then burst out laughing. "Only David Canfield would be so arrogant as to bring me my own flowers as an olive branch."

Her laughter held the same note of delight that had once drifted over the water. David relaxed and let his gaze glide through the room, over the mildly cluttered desk and a lovely collection of pottery, to a small table before a window overlooking the lake. "Your table, it's set for two." Crystal and silver gleamed beneath the candle surrounded by flowers. David rarely bothered with possessions. His life and work forbade it, but he knew simple elegance when he saw it.

"It is, isn't it?" Raven looked up from arranging his flowers, her flowers, in a vase.

"You were expecting company."

"Not expecting. Hoping."

"I don't think you need worry on that score. If it tastes half as good as it smells."

"Are you hungry, David?"

He started to deny it, but decided that if this was to be a new beginning, he would be as honest as he knew how. "My cooking isn't exactly the greatest."

"Then join me."

Surprise leapt in his face. When he crossed the yard, the most he was hoping for was that she wouldn't slug him. "What about the guest you were expecting?"

"Hoping, David," she corrected as she set the flowers on a counter. "I was hoping you would join me for dinner."

"Me! Why?" He couldn't quite believe that she was standing there, more lovely than any woman on earth, asking him to sit at her table as if they were friends.

She looked at his flowers and smiled again. "Shall we call it my peace offering?"

"You knew I was coming over?"

"That was the last thing I expected. When you knocked at the door, I was coming to you."

I was coming to you. The phrase brought a vision that had nothing to do with dinner. He dragged his thoughts back from dangerous ground. "You're asking an arrogant, insulting bastard to have dinner with you?"

"No. I'm asking the man who brought me flowers." She put her hands on her hips, pulling the fullness of her caftan close to her body. "Are you going to accept my invitation?"

"If you'll tell me why you bothered."

Raven gestured eloquently, her bosom rising beneath the azure silk. "I think because I like you."

"Why in hell would you like me?" David asked, remembering the insults, the cruelties.

"Only God knows that, and maybe Simon. After all, he sent you here." Raven slid her arm through David's. "When I figure it out for myself, I'll tell you." With a smile that wiped the slate clean and signaled a new beginning, she led him to the table.

Three

David looked over the book he was reading, his gaze following his thoughts to Raven. For an hour, he'd tried to concentrate on a rambling tale of science fiction. The week, this night, Raven, disturbed him. Since the initial dinner, their first real step toward peaceful coexistence, their evenings had become routine. They began with dinner, followed by a stroll by the lake, then desultory conversation until Raven at her easel or he with his book began to droop and yawn.

Routines were dangerous. One became complacent. Restless caution grew tame. The edge that could mean survival was lost. He'd survived the streets, jungle warfare and The Watch by resisting routine.

Until now. Until Raven. She intrigued him. When his guard slipped, she made him comfortable. Mystery and comfort—an intoxicating mix more dangerous than routine.

Tonight, the routine changed. No aimless walk. No conversation. Raven was quiet, shunning her painting for clay. It was the first time she'd worked with the clay at a small, worn potter's table.

As he watched, her flashing fingers shaped the clay like magic. In a pool of light, with shadows playing over her features, she was pensive. The mass took form, and silent tension gradually vanished, as if the clay had drawn it from her. This quiet intensity, the channeling of her strength fascinated him. He'd known her for weeks, and each day, there were new facets, half revealed, half hidden.

It was the mystery that kept drawing him back. Each day, he promised there would be no more of such evenings. Each evening, after a day in the valley without her, he found himself waiting for the invitation he knew would come. And as ever, as tonight, he didn't refuse. Couldn't refuse, he admitted and looked away.

The room was like her. Warm, welcoming, a place to ease one's troubles. A room that gave but did not take. That, too, like Raven.

But what troubles could there be for her in her mountain paradise? he wondered as she set aside her work. "Finished?" he asked, admitting his vast ignorance.

Raven glanced up in surprise, as if she'd forgotten he was there. A shake of her head sent her hair tumbling over her shoulder. "It isn't finished. Tomorrow it will dry in the sun, after that, I'll paint it with a slip."

"Slip?" David laid his book down, more interested in the play of light over her face than in the answer.

"Clay in liquid form," she explained. The clay, smooth and nearly black, bore her signature, the flowering dogwood. "For this, I think, a white slip of kaolin."

"White on black?"

"White on white. Eventually. Before the slip dries, it will be polished with river stones. Then, perhaps I'll paint a design before it's fired, perhaps not. In the firing, the black clay will become white, the kaolin will stay true."

"White on white."

"Yes."

"If you paint it, what design will you choose?"

"The lines of the vessel determine its design."

"Sounds very artistic."

Raven shook her head again. "Not really. Only therapeutic. Working with the clay was one of many things Rhea McKinzie taught me. The table, the tools and the methods I use were hers. When she was troubled, she would sit for hours, working the clay, pouring her worries into it."

"As you did tonight."

Taking a wet cloth from the table, Raven rubbed it over her hands, cleansing the last remnants of clay from them. "Yes," she admitted. "As I did tonight."

"It's hard to conceive that a problem could create something such as this." He gestured toward the clay. The word *pretty* came to mind and was discarded. The work was too strong, too striking to be only pretty. *Handsome* was one description. *Masculine* another. Did her thoughts guide her hands? Was there a man beyond the valley that had driven her to pour her troubles into the clay as Rhea McKinzie had?

David felt something ugly and alien twist in his gut. "Is this man worth so much agonizing?"

Raven followed his gaze, as if seeing the vessel for the first time. It was solid and stark, and if clay could be attributed gender, it was masculine. David Canfield was surprisingly perceptive. "Both men are worth it."

The ugliness lashed at him. Irrational anger rose in his throat like acid, driving him to his feet. *Jealousy!* He drew a slow, deep breath to calm himself. It didn't work. Good Lord! It was true. He was jealous of a stranger. Two strangers. He had to know. "Why? Why do they matter?"

Raven was startled by the hardness of his tone. "The McLachlans are a fine family. Thanks to Dare, the eldest. He raised all three of his brothers. Half brothers," she corrected. "Alone and with unrelenting Scot stubbornness, he made them into fine young men. Now that very stubbornness is threatening to tear the family apart."

"What form does this destruction take?" David's drawl was laced with distaste. "Two men, or worse, two brothers, in love with the same woman?"

"I beg your pardon?" Raven lifted her eloquent hands, gesturing that she didn't understand.

David took a step closer. "That is how it goes, isn't it? The classic triangle, two men, one woman."

"A woman?" Raven was truly puzzled. Then, "I'm sure Jamie could have plenty of women friends or lovers, and so could Dare. But at the moment, their problem isn't a woman. I wish it were that simple."

"What could be more complicated than a woman?"

"Honor. Love. Ambition. One man's dreams for another. Dare's for Jamie. Jamie's a gifted pianist, but he wants nothing more than he wants to be a tree farmer like Dare. Dare won't hear of it. He's determined that Jamie won't throw away his talent. Both are so hot-headed, neither will even try to compromise. Jamie's young. This is his first year at the college. If Dare would just listen.''

"Jamie is a student?" David interrupted. "And his brother, Dare, is a farmer?"

"Jamie McLachlan is eighteen. Dare is thirty-eight. He's the one who should be cooler and wiser."

"A student and a farmer," David said, then he chuckled. "A farmer and a student." The chuckle became laughter, the sound of relief. A pimply faced kid and a grizzled backwoodsman. Laughter dwindled into a grin as his eyes met Raven's.

"It isn't funny," she said mildly. "Dare's a proud man, and he wants more for Jamie than he had himself. He just can't see that Jamie doesn't want it. Not yet. Maybe never. If they can't resolve this or at least call a truce, their brothers, Ross and Robert Bruce, will be drawn into it."

"Why do you care so much, Raven?" Laughter vanished before the onslaught of more primitive emotions.

Raven hesitated. There was something different in his voice. She'd never heard him say her name in quite that way, a tone that made her breath catch in her throat and her mouth go dry. He was moving toward her, his steps deliberate. Nothing had overtly changed. He was the image of easy civility, but with every step, she sensed restless excitement, seething, barely tethered. The air was suddenly charged with it, prickling up and down her skin, setting her heart into a ragged rhythm.

"I care because a family is too precious to stand idly by and watch it be destroyed," she whispered, grasping absently at the original train of her thoughts. What was between them now had nothing to do with Jamie or Dare McLachlan.

He watched her watch him, seeing the tilt of her head, the lifting of her chin, feeling her eyes on his. At the table, he stopped. Her face was turned to him, away from the lamp where she worked. Only her hands were under the light. They were strong and rough, the nails short. Capable hands, talented hands. When she'd risen out of the lake, he had thought her hands did not suit her. Now he knew he was wrong.

Peaceful days and quiet evenings were forgotten, wiped from memory as if they'd never happened. The easiness, the comfort were gone. In their place was seething hunger and desire. "Did you think you would tame me, Raven? Draw me into your life. Feed me. Show me the kind of life I've never had. Will never have." He touched her hand, then drew away. "These aren't the hands of Lilith. Lilith could never have entranced me so."

He made a low, wordless sound. "Do you know how I felt when I thought you were troubled by a lover?" He didn't wait for her answer. He needed none, for it was in her eyes.

His chest rose in a slow, deep breath. His growl held no humor. "You have no idea, do you? Just as you hadn't known—" He broke off abruptly, only to begin again. "You were content sitting with me here, night after night. Too contented to know that you were driving me out of my mind." He traced the line of her cheek. His gaze locked with hers, seeing the knowledge in them. "But you know now, don't you?"

"I know."

She didn't flinch, didn't blush, didn't look away. He wanted to annihilate that rigid control, to see her fevered with passion. "I've fought this, Raven McCandless. From the moment I saw you, I've fought it.

"Night and day. No matter what I did, you were in my thoughts." His hand slid into her hair, gathering it roughly in his fist. "There are times when the only way to win the battle is not to fight anymore."

Then Raven was rising, willingly or with the pressure of his hand, he didn't know which. His mind was too full of the scent of her. He ached too much for the sweetness of her mouth to care.

He felt her shiver, heard the rush of a sigh. As his lips came down on hers, she murmured, "I was never contented."

David's kiss was fierce, demanding. And Raven discovered she could no more reject his demand than she could escape the strong, warm prison of his arms. His hand in her hair tugged her head back, exposing her throat. His mouth was hot as it moved over her tender flesh. He drew her closer, and Raven gasped as every line of his body branded hers. Desire, rampant and new, swept over her. She moved against him, wanting more.

David went very still, not even daring to breathe. Raven turned her head only the little his grasp of her hair would allow. Her lips brushed his in a whisper-soft touch. A low groan shuddered through him, and he kissed her again. His lips slanted over hers, thirsting. Her mouth was sweet wine when she opened it to him.

Raven felt herself falling, spiraling down into a land where she'd never been. Where there were needs stronger than all she believed or thought or wanted. She was afraid, not of David, but of Raven McCandless. She was frightened, but fear was no match for his desperate lust or the desire that had needed only his kiss to awaken. Her hands caught in his hair as she met fury with fury, demand with demand and found them answered. He was wildfire, burning away the last shred of caution. She writhed in his arms, clung to him, whimpered when she could not be a part of him.

"Raven?" Shaken, he took a step back, holding her shoulders, keeping that little distance of sanity. His gaze touched the tangled hair, the bruised, pouting mouth, met the heavy-lidded look of desire. Her breasts rose in a ragged breath, but she didn't look away. She wanted him and couldn't hide it. As he'd wanted her from the first.

He'd tried to despise her for what she was, for the comfortable, parasitic life she represented. He had disavowed his male needs. Each day and each night, he had struggled, fighting himself, Raven and the inevitable. Yet, deep inside himself, he'd known.

He was wrong for her. She for him. He was a disciplined man. His mind ruled his heart and body. Reason over lust. But not now. He could no longer deny himself. He wouldn't fight a battle lost before it began.

Bending, he swept her from her feet. Spinning, he walked to the door he knew led to her bedroom. His foot against it sent it splintering from its latch and colliding with the wall. Stepping inside, he spared no glance for the Spartan comfort that spoke of Raven.

He thought only of a woman more desirable than any. Setting her on her feet, he held her to him, steadying her as she swayed. As he brushed the tangle of her hair from her face, she smiled at him like a sleepy child. In the light of a lamp only as bright as a candle, her eyes were drowsy and full of trust. He almost left her then. He almost walked out her door, out of her valley and her life forever. Until he remembered the lake and moonlight and Raven rising from it like a goddess. Until he remembered her soft whisper.

I was never contented.

The last threads of sanity slipped beyond him as he reached for the first button of her shirt. His finger skimmed her skin in his task, feeling the throb of her heart in every part of her. "You're trembling."

"I know," she murmured, the words catching in a ragged staccato as the last button slipped free and his hands slid beneath the soft fabric to cup her bare breasts.

His fingers were rough, but his touch was gentle. Their slow, soothing stroke taking the weight of her softness, lifting, caressing, always stopping at the verge of her tender, aching nipples. The back of his hands trailed down her sides and over her midriff. His thumb raked the fold where breasts lay gentle over ribs. The fine down on his hands was like a thousand caresses, honing Raven's senses to a razor's edge. The slightest contact sent ripples of excitement quivering through her. He was teasing her. Tormenting her as she wondered wildly how torment could be so sweet.

Raven grasped his shoulders, her nails digging into the heavy muscles for support. Her body arched, her breasts lifted, offering their rose crests to his touch. But David denied her. With his palms, he followed the path he had before. Down her side and over her midriff. The hard, callused palms were hot. They burned a trail over her body, always teasing, never satisfying, driving her further into the madness. She had never needed a man to touch her as she needed David to touch her. She wanted to plead with him for more, but all she could manage was simply, "David."

With his eyes still holding hers, he brushed the long, flowing shirt from her shoulders. In a languid, unhurried motion he let it fall to the floor. Slowly, he stroked her throat, his hand sweeping over her naked shoulders and the sides of her breasts, stopping there, holding their swell. "Lovely Raven," he whispered. "Always so reserved, so untouchable. Until now. Tell me what you want."

Raven couldn't bear his gaze. Her lashes drifted over the dark mystery of her eyes. She was trembling when she cried, "I can't."

His thumbs moved over her breasts, circling the aureole, stroking the hard bud of her nipples. "Is it this, sweet Raven?"

"Yes." She arched against his hands. "Yes."

"Or is it this?" He leaned to her, taking her into his mouth.

Raven had no answer. Her head was thrown back, her curved body undulating with his suckling. The gentle nip of his teeth nearly drove her to her knees. Her grasp strained at his shoulders, her nails flayed his skin. Tomorrow, there would be blisters of blood, like banners, over his shoulders. But Raven didn't know the damage her desperate effort not to fall at his feet had done. "David, please."

His head lifted from her body. His eyes found hers again. As he wiped the sheen of sweat from her forehead, he said again, "Tell me what you want."

With her body cooling from his caress, Raven could only shake her head. "I don't know."

"Don't you, Raven?" He shook her gently. "We both know you're too old to play the innocent."

"I don't know. I don't."

"Stop. If I must play the game to have you," he said roughly, "then we'll play the game."

"No game." Coherent thought was beyond her now. "No game. I've never—"

"Don't." His hand closed over her mouth briefly. "Don't make a fool of yourself. I don't care how many lovers you've had. Not now," he murmured as anger added to the power of his desire. "Not ever."

Raven wanted to speak, to tell him his mistake, but as his head bént to her, she forgot everything but David. Then he was kneeling before her, sliding her jeans from her hips.

"You're a beautiful woman, Raven McCandless. Here." He stroked her breasts lightly, moving quickly away. "And here." He touched her midriff, trailing a fingertip over her navel to the lace of her panties. "And here." His hand moved lower. When Raven shuddered and swayed, he was rising to catch her. "Beautiful women need legions of lovers, worshipers at the shrine of beauty. Tonight, there will be only one."

When Raven was capable of thought again, she was naked, lying on her bed, waiting for David.

He had called her beautiful, cruelly and viciously, making it an insult. As she lay tousled and a little drunk with passion, he regretted his sarcasm. There was an untouched aura about her that even sultry sensuality couldn't tarnish. She was two people. The innocent who trembled as if his touch were her first; the proud siren who stood before him half-clothed, challenging every male instinct. Which woman was she? Either or both, for just this night, she was his.

Lifting the hem of his shirt, he ripped it from his body. He'd loosened his belt when he caught a glimpse of himself in the shadowed mirror over her dressing table. The man he saw bore little resemblance to the David Canfield he thought he knew. His hair was disheveled, his face flushed and grim: the cool chameleon of The Black Watch, driven to madness by a woman.

David was suddenly, unexpectedly afraid for her. Afraid of what a man who had never known gentleness might do to a woman whose life had been nothing else. "Raven." His voice was a rasp, his eyes on the stranger in the mirror. "Stop me. Tell me to go away, and I will."

"I can't tell you to go away." Her voice rose from the bed in a whispery rush.

"Then tell me you don't want me. Before it's too late."

"It's already too late." The truth. Always from Raven.

"I'm mad, Raven. I don't know what I'm doing or what I'm saying." He turned from the mirror, the sight of her sweeping everything from his mind. His hand went again to his belt. A zipper rasped, then he was naked.

He moved from the dark into the light, and Raven gasped. A sliver of moonlight slanted through the window, painting his body with a silver sheen. He was light and darkness. She hadn't known that beauty and such utter maleness could be the same. He called her beautiful, but it was he who was beautiful. Long, lean thighs rippled as he came to her. His chest heaved, drawing the flesh over corrugated abdomen and ribs. David lived hard, worked hard, expecting no reward beyond survival. His body, aroused and hungry for her, was testament to that life. To survival.

This, too, was survival, she thought as he stood by the bed, looking down at her. Without him, here, now, she would surely die. Raven laughed softly at her melodrama, a lovely, irresistible sound as she lifted her arms to him.

He let her draw him down to her, sinking into her embrace. He kissed her, stroked her, meaning to tease and torment. He wanted to drive her as mad as he, shattering completely the cool control. But there was no control to shatter. She was a whirlwind. Untamed, unpredictable, matching him kiss for kiss, caress for caress, tumbling fiercely with him over lavender-scented sheets.

Rising over him, she caught both his hands in one of hers. Holding them captive with only the strength of her wish not to be distracted by his touch, she explored his body. And she watched him as if she were just learning what would please and excite a man. Where her fingers trailed, her lips followed.

He felt the shudder begin in the pit of his stomach, spreading to every nerve and sinew. He was near the end. It was her torment that was complete. Clasping her wrists, he tumbled her to her back. With her hands pinned beside her head he kept them from their lethal forays. "Enough," he growled. Then more softly, "Dear God! Enough!"

"Enough," Raven echoed, her voice unsteady.

He came down to her, his hard body covering hers. He was trembling when he sought the final release. His brutal hunger would hurt her, and in a lucid moment, he knew he must be gentle. With agonizing care that was nearly his undoing, he let the searing heat of her enfold him slowly. Still, Raven recoiled and cried out.

David froze, the motion of his body ceasing. Knowledge, truth, but too late. When he would've drawn away, Raven arched against him and their joining was complete.

"No!" David cried. "Damn you, no." But even as he cursed her, she was drawing him down, moving against him until he was lost. "Damn you." The hoarse chant accompanied the pulsing of their bodies. "Damn you." Exquisite pleasure exploded within him. "Raven."

The moon moved beyond the window, but for the tiny pool of light beneath the lamp, the room was in darkness. They slept and woke, and, exhausted, slept again. Each time they came together, the fever in David grew torrid and Raven's response wanton. As dawn was breaking, sleep for once eluded him. He lay bound to Raven by the web of her hair, staring at the ceiling, wondering what in hell he'd done.

The night replayed in his mind. Every detail, every nuance excruciatingly clear. He saw her body trembling from his touch, and his fingers pulsed with the memory. His lungs were filled with her, his mouth with the taste of her kiss. His body ached in a most satisfying way from his use of hers.

Use. That's what he meant it to be. An exorcism, a cure. A victory. He'd been so certain, he hadn't listened, discounting her protests of innocence before she could make them. He'd been so cruel, so sure, and it hadn't mattered. She'd given herself to him with no restraints, with no questions of the past, no bargaining for the future. In the aftermath, in an unguarded moment, languid with pleasure, she spoke of love.

Love.

The word forced David from her bed. Raven stirred, reached for the space where he'd been, and whimpered in her sleep. He looked down at her, feeling trapped. He didn't doubt her. A woman of thirty, a virgin in a time when virginity meant little, would give it only to the man she loved.

He didn't want her love. Love was a burden, a trap. Sacrifice. He wanted no part of it. None! He wanted to snatch her from the bed and shake some sense into her. He wanted to make her hate him so much, she would forget this foolishness of love. With fists clenched and his naked body taut, he glared down at her. He wanted . . God help him . . . he wanted to kiss her.

"Fool!" The word was a snarl as he snatched his clothes from the floor and stalked from the room.

Raven sighed, stretching every sore limb deliciously. She felt wonderful. No day was as beautiful. So this was what sex was all about. She laughed. If she'd known it was quite like this, she would've tried it long ago. No, she wouldn't, she amended, for she'd been waiting for David.

Rolling into the spot where he'd lain, she pretended she felt his warmth and wished he was with her.

Making love, she thought happily. It was truly that.

She stretched again, loving every ache from sleeping entwined. Though she hadn't wakened when he left her, she had known. Now, she wanted to find him. He'd been away too long.

"Whoops!" She swayed dizzily as she stood and clung to the tall bedpost. Can't be pregnant. Not this soon. Although she knew it was a very real possibility. Precautions were not an integral part of her life. And David hadn't been prepared. She glanced at the clock by the bedside. She could be six or four or three hours pregnant. She grinned beneath a blush at the thought of the times.

A sturdy little boy with David's sherry-colored eyes. A little girl to tease the solemn look from his face. A child. Fruit of their loving. Raven threw back her head and laughed, a happy sound drawn from a perfect world.

Scooping up her shirt from where he'd dropped it, she slipped into it. Not bothering with buttons or worrying that the garment barely reached her thighs, she hurried to David.

He was in her kitchen, sitting on the window seat, staring out at the lake with one knee drawn up, his wrist resting on it. In one hand was a cup of coffee. Dangling between the fingers of the other was a cigarette. She stopped in the doorway, reveling in the luxury of watching him.

He was combed and dressed, his shirt neatly tucked into his jeans, his canvas shoes laced and tied. Untouched, she thought. As if last night never happened. She looked down at her rumpled shirt hanging open over her bare body. It had. She laughed giddily. Very definitely, it had.

He turned at the sound. Raven waited for him to speak. She smiled, but David's solemn face didn't change. Lifting the cigarette to his lips, he inhaled and exhaled slowly. Through a haze of smoke, he watched her. Raven felt that stare as if it were his caressing hand. Pavlovian desires. David looked; she responded. A conditioned reflex. A wonderful reflex.

"Good morning," she said at last, certain he could read what she was feeling in her face.

"Is it?" He looked away grinding the cigarette out in the ashtray beside him. When he looked back at her, a trick of the light turned his eyes cold.

"I thought . . ." She hesitated, shaking her head. She didn't know what she thought.

He stood, setting his cup aside, and moved toward her, slowly, stalking his prey. "What did you think,

Raven?'' He asked almost too softly. "That we would fall into bed, then live happily together forever? It doesn't work that way. Not for me. Love!'' He said the word as if it were a curse. "A burden, lady, a trap. It puts responsibility and guilt on people who don't need it. Helen Landon died in a South American jungle because she thought she loved me. I didn't ask for it. I didn't want it.'' He was closer now, and Raven saw the light had nothing to do with the coldness in him. "Just as I didn't want anything from you except a quick tumble between the sheets.''

Raven's throat was dry. She couldn't speak, but if she could, what would she say? She wanted to look away, but his hand suddenly cupping her chin prevented it. The utter contempt she saw in him turned shock to churning sickness. It took every bit of strength, dragged from the bottom of her soul, to face his scorn.

"You were good, baby. The best.'' His lips formed a cruel caricature of a smile as a finger trailed down the edge of her open shirt, drawing a line of fire that nearly took her breath away. His hand splayed over her belly. "Your little surprise means nothing to me. You sacrificed your precious virginity on the wrong man.''

Anger did what shock and pain couldn't. She was glacially calm when she grasped his wrist, drawing his hand from her body. "You knew. I told you.''

"A woman says a lot of things in the heat of the moment.''

"Yes.'' She released his wrist almost nonchalantly. "Particularly when her teacher is as skilled as David Canfield. I won't be so naive next time, with the next man.'' She might have been standing fully clothed, speaking of something as unimportant as a minor disagreement. "I should thank you for the lesson in the etiquette of one-night stands, as well as for relieving me of the burden of virginity. You've taught me how good uncomplicated sex can be. You made me good because you're good," she parroted him. "The best yet, in my limited experience."

"Damn you!" His fists were clenched, not against the cool assessment of his performance, but in mercuric and unreasoning anger at the specter of Raven with another man.

"You've damned me rather thoroughly already," Raven said calmly. Turning from him, she walked to the door and opened it. "If you'll leave, I can get dressed. I have a great deal to do today."

She was magnificent, standing in the doorway. Proud, beautiful, so remote, he wondered if he'd imagined the woman who had been a flame in arms. A strange sadness—for the hurt he caused, for the love he didn't want—tempered his anger. "It would be best if I left the valley, but I gave Simon my word."

"And you always keep your word." She didn't mock him. She had too much class to stoop to mockery.

"Yes," he said simply. Then he felt compelled to add bitterly, "There were times when my word was all I had. If it's of no value, then neither am I."

"Keep your word. Stay in the valley, but leave me."

"Raven . . ."

"No apologies." She was as frigid as a winter night.

"No apology," he agreed. Wondering if it were not he who was damned, he stepped past her and out of her life.

Raven didn't watch him leave. She couldn't. Closing the door on the sight of him, she sagged against the wood. After a moment, the shaking stopped. With her palms flat against the door, she pushed away from it. Collecting herself, she straightened.

She'd been a fool. She faced the fact with the honesty that was as necessary to her life as her heartbeat. She'd given her body and with it, her heart, to a man who hated her. There were many things she would regret—her innocence, his enmity, her reckless assumptions. But not the giving. Never that. No matter how naive she'd been, a part of her knew no man would ever make love to her as David.

"No regrets," she murmured.

Never. Yet there was one thing she must know. Crossing to the telephone, she dialed a number. After a time, without preamble, she spoke into the receiver. "Simon, classified information of The Watch or not, I must know about Helen Landon."

As Simon began to speak, she settled into a chair to listen.

Four

Raven sat before her potter's table. The last of the natural light streamed through the open door. Her idle hands were folded loosely about a polishing stone. A white slip dried, unnoticed, on a clay pot. She'd begun with the intention of readying it for the kiln, but as with all her tasks of late, her hands grew still as her mind drifted. Simon spoke in her thoughts as clearly as he had days ago over the telephone.

Helen Landon? he had repeated, buying time, gathering his thoughts, as Raven had heard him do so often.

Yes, Simon, Helen Landon. She'd been patient. With Simon it was the only way. He would not be hurried.

Then David hasn't told you.

If he had, Simon, I wouldn't be bothering you.

Your voice, from the tone of it... It's not going so good, this thing with David?

She had paused, searching for an easy answer, then settled for blunt honesty. *No.*

I'm sorry, Raven. I didn't mean this.

It's too late for apologies, Simon. Just tell me about Helen Landon.

Then Simon began to speak, not of Helen, but of David as he'd been, as he was.

He was a special kid. Came from a hard-working middle-class family that if it had any luck at all, it was bad. The father's health failed. An expensive illness. Lost his business, his house. Moved to a poor neighborhood, taking nothing but his pride. The mother managed to provide the necessities with nothing left over for their only son's future. No training, no college. But they gave him a good home and instilled in him their old-fashioned ideals. He grew up tough in a tough neighborhood, but their teachings survived. Longer than either of them. David was alone and barely of age for the wind down in Vietnam. He was quick and responsible, and he moved up in the ranks. When he came to my attention, he was still new enough that he continued to cling to his idealism.

When Simon paused, the soft roll of his burr dying away, she prompted him, wanting to hear more. Much more. *He was special, an idealist, and you recruited him for yourself?*

For The Watch. He was the first.

And the best?

Yes, Raven. The best.

An idealist with a conscience. A rare breed for The Watch.

Rare and good. The Watch has a conscience, it must. Most just suspend it at times. But not David. It made him the best—and nearly destroyed him.

She had struggled with anger she had no right to feel. *You had to know what it was doing to him, Simon.*

I knew. I've watched the light go out of his eyes and the smile that could melt hearts disappear. And still, I gave him every ugly assignment.

Because David would do it and do it well, no matter what it did to him. Was it worth it?

Yes. Simon, unequivocally honest to the last.

It was worth a man's soul?

At the time, yes.

And now?

He was quiet for so long Raven had begun to think the connection had been severed. Then she heard a weary sigh and Simon was speaking again.

I wouldn't have done this to him if it weren't worth it.

A gentle rebuke. *I know, Simon. I think I only wanted to hear you say it.*

David's seen terrible things and done terrible things. It takes its toll on a man with his conscience.

As Helen Landon did?

She was young and new to the job, and a little starry-eyed, but she was good. David was the best in the business. As a rule, he worked alone, but this time, he needed a partner. They made a good team.

David said she loved him.

Yeah, I guess she did.

He didn't love her?

Raven had to ask, though she knew the answer.

What happened to David, the disillusionment, the anger, was already brewing. Helen's death was only the catalyst. He would've regretted losing her, but another time, under other circumstances, it wouldn't have thrown him into a tailspin. People die in our business, Raven, and we grieve for a time, then go on.

How could this happen to him?

The answer to that, honey, is because he's David. Simon launched into a narrative of David and all he'd done. As if it were catharsis for his own soul, the story poured out. Raven was concerned, then she realized there were no particulars. Simon was not revealing confidential information. He spoke of accomplishments and their emotional toil, of burnout. He ended with David's last mission.

They were betrayed. The guerillas were waiting for them. Helen was taken prisoner. There was information she could have given them that would harm David.

But she didn't. Even when they hurt her. The love Raven knew he didn't want.

David took her from them. Then he stayed with her.

Until she died. The intolerable sacrifice, leaving unbearable guilt.

Weary regret had roughened Simon's voice. *David came out of the jungle alone.*

Raven hadn't needed specifics. No one had to tell her how terrible it was for Helen. For David, waiting, knowing why she was dying. For Simon who sent her.

It was the last straw, Raven. He turned his back on everything he believed in.

He's going after the one responsible on his own. Beyond the law, if he has to. And you can't stand by and let him do it.

No, if he does . . . Raven, David's only a step away from becoming a renegade. We can't let that happen.

Is that what you do, Simon? Take a man, a special man, exploit him, turn him into a machine. Then when he's in trouble, do you hunt him down like an animal?

Nobody's hunting David down. Not while I'm alive.

David's only trouble is that he feels guilty for living. As you did.

Until you brought me here, and with Rhea, made me see that it wasn't wrong to live. Suddenly, everything had become crystal clear. *That's why you sent him to me, isn't it Simon? To do for him what you did for me.*

She'd heard only his breathing, harsh and slow over the phone lines. He was remembering a dear, dying friend bequeathing a child to him. She had waited, listening to the hollow silence until he found his voice.

Did I do wrong sending him to you, honey?

I don't know.

I can recall him. David keeps his word, but if I release him... Should I, Raven?

She couldn't humiliate herself by asking Simon to call David from the valley because of her foolish infatuation. Nor could she pretend she wanted it for David's sake, not her own. Her damnable honesty wouldn't let her.

No matter how she might want to twist and turn it, convincing herself and Simon that David should leave the valley, it was not possible. Her foolishness and his antagonism aside, David needed the valley. Simon was a wise man. He knew that his best agent needed the valley's peace to heal his mind and find himself. She knew, more by what Simon didn't say than by what he did, that professional help for a man like David could be disastrous. He would be buried in the labyrinth of government hospitals and institutions and never be a concern again. She couldn't let that happen to David.

In the end, she'd gathered her courage and listened to what she wanted to believe was her conscience and knew was truly her heart. *Don't recall him, Simon. I can't help him, but time can. David's strong. He'll mend in spirit as well as mind. He needs the valley. Let him stay.*

Are you sure, honey?

I'm sure.

You'll call me if you need me?

I'll call.

Honey.

Yes, Simon?

Take care.

The conversation surfaced time and again. In the early morning hours spent in her garden. When she drove over the mountains to the college. But most of all, when the day was quiet, she thought of all that Simon had told her of David.

She heard Simon saying, *Take care.* And the echo of her answer.

"It's too late, Simon," she murmured aloud, running a finger over the drying slip. Once her carelessness with it would've disturbed her, but tonight, her mind was too full of David.

David, his face solemn, his eyes brooding. David, laughter transforming his features. His eyes heavy with passion, crying, "Enough!"

What had she been thinking when he took her in his arms? Nothing. She was only feeling as she'd never let herself feel before.

"Let?" She laughed, a mirthless sound. With David, there wasn't a choice. It was simply there, full-blown and aching, beyond control. From the moment he'd stepped out of the darkness, a stranger with a stranger's needs, all she'd learned of protective detachment was threatened. Her world had changed forever beneath the look that turned moonlight into witchery.

Shock had given her brazen courage when she stood naked beneath the nebulous shield of her wet shirt, feigning an outward calm as his scorching stare saw what no man had. With every shred of her strength, she'd faced his challenge. Only when he'd left her, reeling from his insults, had reality crashed down about her.

She hadn't tried to hate him then, nor had she wanted to, for hate implies a compelling awareness. She'd wanted the protection of indifference. Then nothing he said or did could touch her. Aloof, she could be, and controlled, even distant, but she'd glimpsed hurt beneath his hostility, and indifference was beyond her.

When he took her in his arms, half in anger, she hadn't thought of consequences or the future. Had there been a future beyond that moment? God help her, no.

She hadn't thought David would be a part of her life beyond that time. She hadn't thought at all. She'd simply given her heart and body to him.

David wanted one, but not the other and she'd discovered they were one and the same. A package deal. Raven shied away from an admission she was not ready to make.

"So, what do I do?" Drawing herself from her quandary, she began to clear the table of her tools, putting them away in a cabinet. The clay vessel was last. As she lifted it from the table, memories overwhelmed her. Of David watching as she shaped it. Of anger and enmity and passion.

"David." Her hands caressed the clay. Her skin flushed hot with her thoughts as she pressed its cool side to her cheek. A sound, a whispered breath, drew her heavy-lidded gaze to the open door.

He was there by the garden's edge, watching through the twilight. The revulsion she saw sent the clay slipping from her fingers, shattering into clumsy pieces. His icy focus never left her, only his mouth altered, his lips compressing into a grim line. Something was gathering beneath the habitual stillness of this rough, hurting man. Something Raven wanted to understand, but they were locked in a wasteland neither compassion nor lust could breach.

The fragrance of a summer breeze drifted lazily through the doorway, stirring Raven's dark hair. She brushed it away from her cheek, running her hand down the length of it, tucking it behind her shoulder. David's eyes left hers to follow its shimmering fall, and Raven remembered his hands in her hair, guiding her mouth to his kiss, tangling himself in it as he made love to her. Bound by it in sleep.

Everything blurred, and there was only the wanting.

Oh, God! Even his hate couldn't keep her from it. Trembling she waited until his uncompromising gaze took hers again, seeing the memory in them. In the hush, his breath rasped in his chest, his hands curled. His eyes were narrow slits, but in their dark glitter, Raven saw an answering hunger that neither hate nor contempt could silence. Primitive lust. Controlled by incredible effort.

The color drained from her face. She looked down at her hands, only their brutal clasp with nails scoring her palm kept her from reaching out to a man who would take her in hate. Wildly, she asked herself if she would go to him, giving whatever he asked, taking like a starving woman any crumb he would give.

"Yes!" She had no idea she spoke her shame as her breath became a racking shudder. God help her, yes. She would do whatever David asked her to do. Be whatever he wanted her to be. All he need do was touch her and she wouldn't have the strength to deny him.

From the far reaches of her mind, she heard Simon saying, *Take care.*

And her own answering, *Too late.*

It was too late the moment David had kissed her.

I love him! The words were startling at first. She'd never deliberately spoken them even to herself. I love him, she admitted again, and this time, there was no doubt. She was nearly giddy with the admission. The insanity of loving him she could cope with. Better than the shame of obsession.

Even as she knew his gaze was on her, hot and hard and full of the need he wanted to deny, she felt the resurgence of her confidence. She loved him and could deal with it. She wouldn't fool herself that it would be easy. But she'd loved before, not like this, not the love of a woman for a man, but love nevertheless. She'd lost before and very nearly not survived it, but she was older now. Perhaps, she would be hurt, perhaps, she would never love again, but she would survive.

With sudden clarity, the complexities were reduced to simple truths. Raven loved David. That was her problem. How he dealt with it was his.

When she lifted her gaze to his, the serenity of old was shining in them. There was a soft strength in her that nothing could extinguish.

David was caught by her gaze, held captive by her smile. He was barely aware of flowers dipping and swaying before a mischievous breeze. Why was he there, lurking in her garden, hoping to catch a glimpse of her?

Why did he torment himself with memories of Raven, hair as black as night veiling her body, turning to him with an honesty he wouldn't believe?

She smiled at him across the night, and a knife turned in his heart. He had brought the ugliness of his life with him into her valley. When he had found peace, he had turned it to discord. When he had found innocence, he had taken it, discarding it like a cheap thrill. Her smile was his punishment.

His fingers curled around the head of a flower, crushing it. The scent of it—her scent—sang in his blood. Ripping the delicate bloom from its stem as if ripping her from his mind, he turned away.

When he was gone, Raven knelt to gather the shattered clay.

The sun struck midday as David drove down the mountain. Beneath shrinking shadows, one steep, hairpin curve plummeted into the next, zigzagging around and down. The sleek Corvette, his one folly, old enough to be a classic and well preserved, hugged the road and clung to curves. When the terrain flattened and twists became lazy bends, he leaned back, put the accelerator to the floor and let the beat of the wind sweep the clutter from his mind.

He'd been isolated too long. Ennui blunted his senses and warped his values. As the Corvette hurled through the gently rolling countryside, he convinced himself that the malady called Raven only needed perspective. She was beautiful, and the tragedy of Helen Landon had shaken him but not gelded him. He was a man with a man's needs, and Raven was there. It was as simple as that.

"The only game in town," he muttered, and hated himself the moment the words were out. It cheapened her, and she didn't deserve that. He cheapened himself by stooping to that way of thinking. Whatever Raven was, she wasn't a game.

Solitary farmhouses surrounded by lush gardens and close-cropped pastures gave way to the clutter of congregate living. David brought his speed under the sedate requirements and drove the streets of Madison, the little village that had grown up around Madison College, where Raven taught.

There were phone booths closer to the valley. He could've called Simon from any of them. But the wanderlust had seized him and without conscious plan, he'd found himself passing them by in favor of Madison.

The village was small, with no industry beyond that expected to serve the immediate needs of the college. Main Street circled a courthouse, and tucked along the street's length were the shops with quaintly refurbished facades. There was a richness here, a quiet sense of worth. A gallant old lady wandering into the twentieth century, teaching it the true meaning of *class*.

Beyond the cluster of houses, some old as the village itself, some new, lay the college itself. A luxuriant expanse of lawn surrounded it, with a forest at its back, and beyond that, the rise of mountains.

It was here Raven spent her days. Within its buildings, she taught her classes of horticulture and her specialty of wildflowers. In the peculiar camaraderie of the academic atmosphere, she interacted with her colleagues and with students and their families—like Jamie McLachlan and his brother Dare.

This was a part of her life David hadn't imagined. He thought Raven aloof, solitary. Yet, as he stopped, staring out at the buildings, he could see her standing before a lectern, speaking to a class. Or bending to a student, her braid tumbling over her breasts like a rope of silk. He'd never imagined Raven in a setting beyond her valley. Now, he knew she would do very well. Her quiet serenity would be appealing. The students would turn to her with their troubles, as Jamie McLachlan obviously had.

The McLachlans. Raven's troubled friends. Raven's caring. Raven rising from her potter's table. Raven in his arms.

Raven.

The sun bore down, turning the black car into an oven. David sighed. He'd come to Madison to make a safe call to Simon, not to moon over a woman he wanted desperately to purge from his thoughts. It was time to get on with his task. If anything could usurp Raven's memory, it should be the investigation.

Reaching for the ignition, he listened as the powerful engine roared. As he left the college behind and retraced the quaint streets, he reminded himself that Madison, with its aura of history and tradition, was not for the likes of David Canfield.

He found the perfect phone booth tucked on a side street beyond the sleepy bustle of the village. His coins clanked into the machine, the number was dialed, and on the second ring, the call was answered, as he knew it would be, by Simon. Dispensing with formalities, David went straight to the point.

"Anything new?" His voice rang hollowly in the cave of metal and Plexiglas. He listened as Simon outlined the progress of his own investigation. "That's it? Zip? Then we aren't dealing with an amateur. This guy's a professional, not just some fly-by-nighter looking for quick bucks. A mole so well placed, he might be anybody. He'll be dangerous, Simon.''

A heavy motorcycle passed, the deep thrum of its motor obscuring Simon's answer. ''Say again.''

When Simon had finished outlining his strategy, David felt a little less cut off from the world he knew. ''One other thing.'' He tugged the number from his pocket. ''I discovered this in the telephone logs.'' He repeated the number. He wasn't ready to admit to Simon that he'd found it days ago and had forgotten it in his preoccupation with Raven. ''When you trace it, get back to me. I can be at this number whenever you say.'' He rattled off the number listed above the dial. ''It's small, but this could be the lead we need.

''Meet you at the what?'' A second motorcycle passed, this one lighter, with an annoying buzz for an engine. The rider, like the first, had books strapped to the seat. College kids? Lunch break at Madison? David leaned forward, the receiver tight against his ear, a hand cupping the other. ''What games?'' He wondered why Simon suddenly wanted to make face-to-face contact when the telephone would suffice. ''Highland Games? Is that where grown men wear skirts and if I yelled, 'Mac,' every damn man in the country would answer?''

He laughed. ''I know, including you. How will I recognize you? Will you be wearing a skirt?'' He held the phone away from his ear until Simon had finished his diatribe, then sobered instantly when he moved on to other subjects. ''Raven's fine, Simon. Yes, I've seen her, but not today. It was yesterday. And yes, she is a special lady.''

As if it were fate and some force had ordained it, while he listened to Simon extol Raven and her virtues, a young woman, slender, with midnight hair flowing down her back stepped from a shop. Her arms were loaded with books, a bag with the name of the shop emblazoned on it swung from her wrist. David's attention wandered from Simon. Would it be this way for the rest of his life? Would every slender, dark-haired woman be Raven in his imagination? Would every graceful walk be hers?

As she drew nearer, her features were blurred. He wiped the sweat from his brows and saw that the woman's hair was like Raven's because it was Raven.

"I'll be at the games. Just have the number." He cut Simon off in midsentence and replaced the receiver. The booth was like an oven, yet he stayed until she passed. Perhaps he intended to let her go, perhaps he was only gathering his courage to face her scorn. He didn't stop to analyze as he stepped from the booth.

"Raven." She stopped, and for an eternity, it seemed she wouldn't turn. When she did, her face was composed, unreadable. He was suddenly at a loss for words, wondering why he'd brought this on himself. She tilted her head curiously, waiting with a maddening patience for his next move. "You left early this morning."

"I had some extra preparations to do for today's class." Her answer was noncommittal, giving him the barest essentials, nothing to ease his malaise.

In the bright sunlight, shadows of restlessness lay beneath her eyes. "Are you all right?"

"I'm as I was yesterday and the day before. As I will be tomorrow. Why do you ask?"

"I thought . . . I worried . . ."

"That I was pining away for my lost virginity?" She was so calm, so matter-of-fact, he wanted to shake her.

Instead, he watched as she smiled again almost pity-ingly. "I'm not, you know. I don't regret it."

He felt as if his heart was in a vise, constricting the flow of his life. He struggled for a breath. "For the love of God, Raven—"

"What were you doing here, David?" she said, cutting him off.

He glanced at the booth and for a moment, his mind was blank. Then he remembered. "I was speaking to Simon."

"I see."

Sunlight glittered in her hair like black diamonds. David could feel its strands drifting over him as she'd learned his body with her lips. Like gentle rain that follows the thunder, he thought, and he lost the thread of his conversation. Raven was speaking, and he had no idea what she had said. "I'm sorry. What did you say?"

She laughed softly. "An apology, David?"

"A courtesy."

Her mouth quirked in a way that made him want to kiss it until it was swollen and sweetly aching. "Is there anything new with the investigation?"

"A lead, maybe." This was solid ground, something he understood. "I won't know until Simon checks it out."

"It must be hard."

"It's damn near impossible." Impossible not to for-get every resolution, that this was a public street and his desire to sweep her into his arms.

"You must feel cut off from everything. I can un-derstand how you must hate it."

She was talking about the investigation. The farthest thing from his mind. "Simon will do his best while I'm in exile."

"Is that how you see it, David? As exile?"

"No. Yes. I suppose I do."

"I know how it feels to be away from the place you want or even need to be. I'm sorry."

"Apology, Raven?"

She laughed, caught in her own trap. "No, only a figure of speech."

Her laughter died as they stood in the burning day. A child with a jam box on his shoulder scooted by them, the mellow refrain of a love song drifting from its speakers. A mournful voice sang of a love that almost was, then faded away. The town clock chimed three-quarters of the hour and fell silent.

"I have to go," Raven said. "I have an appointment."

"I'll carry your books." David took a step toward her and for the first time her control crumbled.

"No!" She backed away a careful step. "They aren't heavy and I'm sure you have something you should be doing."

"There's nothing." He advanced another step.

"David, no!"

He heard the thread of panic. He stopped, his hand outstretched until, feeling like a fool, he dropped it.

"I'm used to the books. They aren't as heavy as they look. I'm late." She backed away another step. "I have to go."

She turned abruptly and walked from him, head down, her books clutched to her breasts. She'd been the epitome of calm control until she thought he would touch her. Then she looked at him as if he were a rattlesnake.

"After what you've done to her, what did you want, Canfield? For her to fall into your arms?"

He watched her move, her body taut, the easy grace gone, and he knew that it was exactly what he'd wanted once. When she turned the corner and disappeared from sight, he felt a sense of loss.

Five

On Saturday, David rose early and dressed in khaki slacks and a light, knit shirt. This was the day he was to rendezvous with Simon at the Highland Games, set in a meadow high on a mountain side. It could take all day. Simon hadn't given David a time; he'd simply said "Be there."

In Madison, after the fiasco on the street with Raven, David had heard talk of the games. They were the topic in every store or shop. The biggest assemblage of clans was expected. The best athletes, the best dancers and pipers. Hotels and motels for miles around had been booked to overflowing for months in advance. He'd begun to understand how popular the event was.

He spent his evenings alone now. They were dull and endless as he systematically worked his way through Simon's library. Last night, he'd selected a number of volumes on the Scots, their tartans, their kith and kin, and their migration to America. As he steeped himself in their traditions, he learned that *mac,* the part of a great many Scottish names, meant simply "son." As did the more obvious *son,* tagged to end of names. Clan was the name given kinsmen united under a chief. Septs were an extension of the clans.

Highlanders, whether American or Scot, could trace their ancestry to a clan. Each clan had its distinctive tartan, or plaid. He read of their bloody history and stubborn survival. These macs and sons brought their pride and endurance with them wherever they roamed. The highlanders of the Carolinas were no exception.

Was Raven the descendant of a son of Candless? Was Simon son of Kinzie? David discovered his own second name was Scot. Sutherland, his mother's people—without a "mac" or a "son," but still a clan with a plaid of red and blue and green. He felt the pride of belonging before he shook it off and called himself a fool. He knew nothing of Scots or clans. He belonged nowhere and to no one. His interest was simply the studying he always did, readying for an unfamiliar situation.

Slipping his watch over his wrist was the last detail before leaving. Giving the room a cursory glance, he opened the door and stepped outside.

The sun was barely lighting the horizon, leaving the valley in unrelieved darkness. Raven hadn't come home last night. Her cabin crouched in the blackness as empty as a lost soul. The valley was dismal without her, and he wondered, as he had through the night, where she'd stayed and with whom.

"Why should you care, Canfield?" His voice was an intrusion in the hush of predawn. He missed her, dammit. Though they hadn't spoken in days, he missed her. Hell! he even missed the dogs.

With an angry fist, he pounded the railing by the steps, wondering why he couldn't get her out of his mind. If he didn't leave the valley soon, he would be a candidate for an asylum. With that bleak thought, he stepped into his car. As he made the two-hour drive, he rehearsed his argument for his release from his word and for his departure from the valley with the little grace he had left.

David moved with the crowd, letting its momentum take him through the gates, past booths with displays of Scottish food and wares, to the meadow. A thread of excitement ran through the people as they sprawled over the hillside on lawn chairs and blankets. A piper band struck up a tune. The shrill caterwaul of the bagpipes grated on his ears, then he caught the tune and the rhythm and decided he liked it. On the field below, men in kilts ran through practice paces, warming up for their events. But David searched the ever-changing crowd for Raven.

His eyes skimmed over the gathering so thick with the tartan, one could mistake it for Scotland. Would she be here? Wasn't every red-blooded Scot for miles around?

"*Ceud mile failte.* Welcome to the Highland Games." Simon stood at David's side, his burr more pronounced than David had ever heard. "It's a fine crowd, isn't it?"

"A fine crowd," David agreed. But where was Raven? Where was she last night?

"Have you ever seen the games?" Simon steered him through the mass, talking as easily as old friends who'd met by accident.

"Never."

"Then you have a treat coming." A band, dressed in velvet jackets and kilts and tall, furred hats, marched past in cadence. The leader called a signal, the pipes wheezed and began to play. "Do you like the pipes?"

"I could learn to."

"Last night, there was a piper's concert and the country dance. I should've told you, but I suppose Raven did."

"I haven't spoken to Raven." David caught Simon's quick, questioning look. "She wasn't home last night nor this morning. Maybe she was here for the concert and dance."

"I imagine she was. Have you seen her yet today?"

"Not today."

"You've quarreled."

"Yeah," David said shortly. "We've quarreled."

"I see." Simon, sometimes the diplomat, dropped the subject. The hand that rested lightly on David's shoulder tightened and steered him into the trees, beyond notice. In the protection of the shadows, he drew a small, white square from his pocket and held it out to David. "The name that matches your number."

David took the scrap from him. This could be the first concrete step toward finding the person or persons responsible for Helen's death. He unfolded the paper, read it, then looked back at Simon. "Jeter? The number called from Helen's desk belonged to Thomas Jeter?"

"An unlisted number."

"Helen had Jeter's unlisted number?"

"Someone who called from Helen's desk had Jeter's unlisted number," Simon corrected.

"There was no one except the three of us in the office at the time the call was made. I didn't make it. I know you didn't. Why on earth would Helen?"

"Maybe she had a thing for Jeter."

"A thing for The Watch's best enemy?"

Simon shrugged his bearlike shoulders. "Maybe she was returning Jeter's call. Maybe he had a thing for her."

"Yeah. Like a cold fish does for a flower."

"A strange analogy."

"A stranger alliance," David growled.

"If there was one." Simon didn't need to tell him that a full-scale investigation was underway nor that Helen Landon's most innocent contact would be probed.

"Who's heading it up?"

"I am, David. If Jeter's involved, then we know he wasted her to get to me."

"Enemy mine."

"Believe it. Before, it was only petty stuff."

It was on David's tongue to ask Simon to release him from his promise. It was the opportune time. If he left the valley, he could help in the investigation. He let it pass. Surprised, he shrugged, saying, "Why have you come, Simon? You could've given me the name over the phone."

"I wanted to see for myself how you are."

"Checking me out?" David asked. Simon wanted to be right, wanted to vindicate his decision not to slap him into the debriefing and treatment center. "Now that you have?"

"Now that I have—" Simon patted his shoulder "—let's go see the games. The opening ceremonies are about to begin, and there's Raven. Shall we join her?"

David turned, meaning to refuse, until he saw her sitting under the shade of an oak. She was dressed in a creamy blouse with leather laces at the neck and a dark, pleated skirt sashed with a length of plaid. Her hair was drawn back from her face in a loose coil low on her nape. She was composed and elegant. Untouchable. He wanted to slide the laces from her blouse and the pins from her hair and take the quiet elegance for his own.

He wanted things he couldn't explain, things he hadn't meant to want. He looked at her now and the slow burn of anger began. Raven was not alone. His eyes narrowed fractionally against the glare. His voice was guttural. "Who the hell is that?"

With a flicker of amusement, Simon glanced at David, then away. "The dark one with Raven? That's Dare McLachlan."

"The farmer." David stared at the broad-shouldered man who sat by Raven. There was a lean hardness about him that neither lacy ascot nor kilt could soften. The farmer leaned closer to Raven, hair as dark as hers brushing her cheek, as he listened to her low comments.

"Dare's a tree farmer," Simon elaborated. "You've met him, then, have you?"

"No," David said shortly. "What the devil is a tree farmer?"

"Christmas trees."

"Christmas trees?"

"The green things we hang tinsel on in December."

David ignored Simon's teasing. "He looks rough for a *tree* farmer." Dare McLachlan had the tight, watchful look David had seen on his own face many times.

"Don't kid yourself that it isn't grueling work."

A younger version of Dare climbed the embankment. With a swashbuckler's grand gesture, he kissed Raven's hand then dropped at her feet. David clenched his teeth as Raven's laughter drifted to him.

"That's Jamie. There's none like him, though he's a twin. Robert Bruce." Simon nodded to an astonishingly handsome boy with silver-brown hair slipping easily by Raven's side. "He's only seconds older than Jamie, and quieter. But when he's into mischief, he has no equal."

"The other brother?"

"Ross is Madison's pediatrician. He'll be along later. Where there's one McLachlan, there's usually four."

"Raven says there's trouble between Dare and Jamie."

"Not surprising. They're too much alike."

David looked doubtfully from Dare's still, somber face to Jamie's flashing grin.

"Dare was the master plan for Jamie at eighteen. He was a rascal, full of the devil himself. The pride and bane of his grandmother who raised him. She died when he was twenty, within the week, he discovered he had three half brothers. His errant dad reappeared, tried to establish himself as the true heir to the farm. Intended to sell it, pocket the money and run. The boy fought him, wouldn't let his dad set foot on the farm. Dare intended to keep it intact. He dropped out of college, took his brothers—that his dad was only too glad to give up—and raised them by himself.

"Ross was eleven. Robert Bruce and Jamie were less than a year. Of the four, only the twins have the same mother." Simon chuckled at his remark. "Of course, they would. They were a wild, motherless lot, and Dare became everything to them. A sobering experience for any daredevil.''

''Jamie wants to be a farmer.''

''And Dare opposes it. It figures. He wants his brothers to have what he missed.''

''Whether they want it or not.''

''No problem with Ross. He wanted to be a doctor from the first. Robert Bruce is a scholar. Jamie's another matter.''

They were a handsome family, brawny and confident. The one aloof, brooding, the others with a hint of mischief in their slanting smiles. They were totally male, as comfortable in their laces and pleated kilts as in jeans and boots.

Dare touched Raven's shoulder and she didn't shrink away. David's envy fanned the flame of jealousy.

''If you can quit glowering, we might join them,'' Simon suggested.

''The blanket's already a little crowded.''

''Won't be for long.'' Not bothering to wait for his consent, Simon led David past other blankets and clusters of lawn chairs to Raven. ''When the games start, the McLachlans will be on the field. Dare throws the caber.''

''Of course! The caber.'' David refused to ask.

''Simon!'' Raven jumped to her feet. ''Simon.'' There was a happy lilt in his name. ''I thought I was dreaming.'' She flung her arms about him. ''Why didn't you tell me you were coming? When did you arrive? How long can you stay?''

Simon laughed and kissed her forehead. ''Taking it in order. You aren't dreaming. I wanted to surprise you. Just a while ago. Only today.'' He looked at her cheeks, flushed with the sun, and ignored the telltale signs of fatigue. "As beautiful as ever and still as popular with the boys, I see." As she stepped out of his arms, he nodded a greeting to the McLachlans, who had stood when she did.

"We nearly had a family feud deciding who got to bring her to the games, Simon." Jamie grinned at Raven. "To keep peace, we all did."

Dare caught a loose strand of Raven's hair and gave it a playful tug. "What Jamie isn't admitting is that we needed a referee, and Raven does it best."

"Is that what you want?" David stared pointedly at Dare's hand twined in dark silk. "A referee."

Tension crackled like summer lightning. Deliberately, Dare's level gaze met David's. "Among other things, Mr. Canfield." With a lazy caress, his gaze still locked with David's, his hand slid unhurriedly from her hair. "It is Mr. Canfield, isn't it?"

David only glanced at Dare's kilt, down and back, but it was enough. "It is *Mister* McLachlan, isn't it?"

"David!" Raven's shock was lost in Simon's laughter.

"You can't insult him that way, David." Simon was still chuckling. "Any Scot who's worn a kilt has heard that old saw. If you really want to make it a day for clichés, ask him what he wears under it."

"What *does* he wear under it?"

Dare's lips quirked in what might have been a smile. "Whatever I choose or don't choose." Eyes as chilled as a mountain lake took David's measure and dismissed him. Turning to Raven, Dare touched her cheek lightly, tracing it to the hint of a cleft in her chin. Ignoring her sudden blink of surprise, he leaned nearer, saying in a tender tone, "I'll see you at nine for the

Tartan Ball." His husky voice dropped a level. "Look pretty for me."

Without a glance at David and only a nod for Simon, he started down the hill toward the field.

Jamie's wicked laugh faded abruptly to surprise. Robert Bruce choked before he discovered an inordinate interest in a blade of grass. Even Simon made an event of clearing his throat. David was only aware that Raven's eyes were bright and glittering and her sunflushed cheeks were brightened more by a blush.

"Canfield." Dare stood halfway down the incline, one foot on a small outcropping of stone. Oblivious of the watching spectators, he waited until David forced his attention from Raven. When their eyes locked, his shoulders tensed, the snowy silk shirt straining over them. His teeth flashed white in his tanned face. "If you've a problem to work off, the wrestling is open to all comers."

His eyes held David's for a fraction too long to be anything but a challenge. "The stakes can be something we both want, Canfield. The first dance with Raven. If Raven agrees." He didn't wait for her comment. "Scots are hospitable people. Perhaps we can find you a clan to represent."

"My mother was a Sutherland," David said with a quiet dignity, and the challenge was taken.

"A good clan." For the first time, Dare's smile touched his eyes, and as quickly, it was gone. "Rob, Jamie." He was suddenly the brother patriarch, the chieftain of the McLachlans. "You have more to do than pester Raven." He waited while the younger McLachlans grudgingly admitted he was right, stole a kiss from Raven and said their goodbyes. With no more concern for David, Dare went with his brothers to the meadow.

Raven had stood quietly during the exchange, but her stillness was deceptive. She was disturbed by the attention caused by the bristling encounter. She was angry and puzzled. Angered by David, who rejected everything she was, who wanted to want nothing from her. Puzzled by Dare, who had little time for women, to whom she was a favored friend, no more or less.

David and Dare were men of different backgrounds but of the same mold. Terse, aloof, sober, single-minded. *Unreasonable.* While she wouldn't have expected geniality, she hadn't anticipated that in her company, they would bristle like stiff-legged dogs snarling over a bone.

It made no sense. They'd acted like children and had made her feel a fool. Only the smirks and twitters of those watching had kept her from stalking away.

The crowd watched now with a collective grin, waiting for the next comic episode. She had no intention of supplying them further amusement.

Raven reined in her temper, denying herself the wonderful pleasure of blistering David with it. Her smile was pleasant, her voice steady, but her eyes flashed as she tucked her arm through Simon's. "I've lost my escorts for the duration of the games. Would you care to join me?"

David opened his mouth but before he could snap out his objection, he heard Simon saying, "We'd be delighted." Then pointedly, "Wouldn't we, David?"

"No."

"Join me, David." Raven gripped his arm, her fingers digging into his flesh. Her smile curved over clenched teeth. "Pretend we're really one happy group. It's the least you can do after making a spectacle of us."

"I didn't make a spectacle. Your boyfriend did that."

"My boyfriend?" Raven's lashes fluttered down in weary disgust. Then regaining her equilibrium, with a subtle wickedness, she looked from David to the meadow. Her gaze searched for Dare and found him. As she watched him lift a weight, arms straining, muscles defined by sunlight and shadow, she murmured softly, "I wouldn't call Dare a boy."

Simon was having trouble with his throat again. David glanced at him but read nothing in his determinedly expressionless face.

"I'm tired of standing, and we're blocking the view. If you care to join me, David, fine. If not, fine." Raven turned to Simon. "You will, Simon? Please?" She stepped to the blanket, gathered her skirt about her and sat. With a Cheshire Cat smile twitching his lips, Simon joined her and, after a moment of indecision, so did David.

With his shoulders brushing hers, he sat stiffly through the opening ceremonies and the march of the clans. Though he reminded himself it was ridiculous, that he came from nowhere, belonged to no one, he felt an odd flicker of curiosity and pride at the passage of the Sutherland clan. With their standard high and kilts swinging, they marched to the beat of a snare.

Simon, who was enjoying everything immensely, leaned over to speak across Raven. "Your clan, David."

"Hardly," he retorted, lapsing into silence as the parade of tartans ended and the contests began.

The day grew hotter, the competition fiercer. The throng was enthusiastic and vocal. There was bedlam about them, but David hardly heard it. He was conscious of the brush of Raven's shoulder against his, of her stillness. The wildflower scent of her was driving him to desperation. She watched the games raptly, cheering a name that fell on his ears in a dissonant note.

The McLachlans were joined on the field by the fourth brother. Ross, like his brothers, was a varying version of the eldest and handsome in his own way. But it was Dare who commanded attention. Bared to his kilt, his body gleaming with a sheen of sweat, he went with seeming ease from one event to the next. David grudgingly admitted Dare was a superb athlete. He was among the best at throwing the weight, and putting the stone, both contests of skill and strength. Now it was time to throw the log that was the caber.

"Perfect," Raven said, judging Dare's throw.

"The red-headed guy threw it farther."

"Distance isn't the point, David." Her tone was cool and steady.

"Then what is the point? Why else would a grown man throw a skinned tree?"

"The goal is a 'twelve o'clock' throw, with the log landing perpendicular to the starting line."

"I suppose McLachlan's an expert?"

"As a matter of fact, he is."

"David," Simon interrupted. "I'd like something to drink, and these old bones are tired. Would you?"

With a look that asked since when did Simon have tired, old bones, David stood and walked away without a word.

When David was lost in the crowd, Raven turned to Simon, accusing, "You're enjoying this."

Simon's smile got the better of him, spreading over his craggy face. "I can't deny it."

"Would you tell me what's enjoyable about two grown men acting like children fighting over a toy?"

"You make a lovely toy, my dear."

"Stop it, Simon. You know that Dare has absolutely no interest in me beyond friendship. For some unfathomable reason, he was pretending."

"David's arrogance got his dander up. I know it, you know it, but David doesn't."

"This is ridiculous. David doesn't even like me. Why should he be jealous, no matter how strangely Dare acts?"

"Why, indeed."

Raven leaned away from him for a long, sweeping look. "You really are pleased with this."

Simon sobered. "Strange as it seems, David's being so disgruntled with Dare is a good sign. It means he's beginning to feel again. I don't fool myself that he's not a bit longer from total recovery, but it's a start. For a long time, he had no room for anything in his life but retribution. Helen Landon was the catalyst. Years of stress and guilt crashed down on him. She's become the focus of an obsession that could've been dangerous to the country as well as himself. Obsession clouds judgment. So does revenge. There's no room for the first in our business, and to survive, we must be above the other."

"I don't understand."

"There are sensitive situations. One wrong move could bring disaster. David—" Simon stopped, at a rare loss for words. He stared into Raven's eyes, willing her to understand what he hadn't said. "David became a threat. There were certain factors who wanted the problem solved."

"These factors, they wanted David locked away?"

"No, Raven," Simon said gently.

Her hands were clasped in her lap. Fear shadowed her eyes. "Dear God," she whispered. "They want David killed!" She looked away, unable to bear the truth. "You sent him to the valley to buy him some time."

"Can you see why today has been good? It might've been unpleasant, but it was beautifully normal. I knew this could be hard on you, honey, but I believed David deserved a chance." He covered her hands with one of his. "God forgive me, I've played havoc with your life."

He touched her chin, lifting her face toward him. He saw the loveliness frayed by strain. "I can send him away."

"Back to them?"

"Not yet. There are other places. Perhaps I should've sent him to one in the beginning."

"But you didn't." Raven knew the "places," as Simon called them, were sanitariums where David's mind would be poked and prodded, and, even with the best of intentions, dehumanized. "You couldn't. Just as you couldn't send a fourteen-year-old girl."

"No."

Raven remembered his gentleness with the wild, bitter creature she'd been. When he cupped her cheek to turn her face to his, she smiled.

Simon studied her features, his gaze moving slowly over them. Raven smiled, but there was always sadness buried so deep in her eyes that only those who loved her, as he did, could see. He wondered if he only imagined he saw a new sadness there, one too new and difficult to be hidden. "I came to see about David, but most of all, I had to reassure myself about you. About what I might've done to you."

"You haven't done anything to me, Simon."

He met her level gaze, probing for his own answers. His hand fell away from her face and onto the blanket. "Haven't I?"

"I'm a woman, not a fourteen-year-old girl. I made a choice." She lifted her head, looking to David, winding his way over the hillside. "Whatever was done, I did to myself."

Simon heard the courage and the pain. He heard resignation as well. "I can still send him away."

"No."

"Do you know what you're saying, lass?"

She watched David approach, soft drinks in hand. He paused. As if he heard a silent call, his head came up, his shoulders straightened. He turned to the field below and met Dare McLachlan's waiting stare.

Raven ceased to breathe. The crowd vanished. The clamor of voices faded. She was locked away from the world. Waiting. Waiting for David's answer to Dare's new challenge.

He was motionless, a somber figure against the backdrop of the color-spattered slopes. It's a game, Raven thought. Only a game that men sometimes play. Dare was a friend. His challenge had nothing to do with her beyond that she was the reason for David's surly hostility. David, though it made no sense, couldn't bear that another man might have what he didn't want.

David wanted to walk away from her, and he'd tried. Perhaps now, he thought, by refusing this foolish challenge, he could. His diamond-hard stare burned across the meadow. He remembered Dare's hand on Raven. A cup nearly collapsed in the crush of his grip, spilling soda over his wrist. Almost imperceptibly, he nodded. Dare McLachlan, feet planted wide, bare chest heaving in a bark of silent laughter, nodded, too.

Raven sighed, reminding herself for the third time that it was only a game. It meant only that David hadn't conquered his desire for her. But even that was better than indifference.

Indifference offered no hope. Desire could become many things.

She was not smiling as she turned back to Simon, but he saw a difference in her. The bleakness was tempered. In a heartbeat, an emptiness was filled by hope and he saw the Raven of old. His worries were easing, his guilt lifting when she took his hand in hers.

"You've taught me to survive," she said. "Whatever happens, I'll be all right." She looked from Simon to David. "Don't send him from the valley. Not yet."

Six

The meadow, once lush and thick, had begun to wear thin when David walked onto it. The games had taken a toll on the grass, more so than on the athletes. These gladiators, who traced their lineage to the clans, were hard, tough men. They wore their plaids with a quiet pride. Jamie McLachlan had scrounged a kilt of the Sutherland clan. Careful not to give offense, David refused to wear it. He chose to wrestle dressed as he was, removing only his shirt and his shoes.

Excitement ran high among the clansmen. Dare McLachlan was a champion wrestler. This dark stranger was an unknown quantity. David heard muffled comments from the Sutherland clan, followed by an approving inspection. He had honed down to sinew and muscle. He looked like exactly what he was, cat quick, agile and strong. It promised to be a memorable match.

A hand came down on his shoulder, a deep, slightly burred voice asked, "Do you know highland wrestling?"

David looked into an austere face topped by auburn curls. The taller man offered his hand. "Patrick McCallum."

"David Canfield." He doubted there was a man on the field who didn't know his name. "I've wrestled, but not highland style."

"Dare asked me to teach you the moves and the rules."

David had seen this Patrick McCallum in the games. When Dare chose a tutor, he chose the best. David looked across the field to the handsome Scot and his brothers.

Following his thought, Patrick said succinctly, "Dare is nothing if not fair."

David wondered suddenly what he was doing here, facing a man simply to assuage his jealousy over a woman he didn't want. Dare McLachlan would be good for Raven. They would make a handsome pair. He remembered Dare's hand twining in her hair. Silk and iron.

No!

The word screamed like a jigsaw through his skull.

Patrick's voice intruded. "Step to the side, beyond the circle, and we'll begin."

David's schooling was short. Patrick McCallum wasted no words, and every move was instructive. When he was done, he considered David's ability. "What you lack in skill, you make up in strength and guts." His grim slash of a mouth lifted in a smile. "You've shown you've plenty of that by coming down to the field." Eyes, blue and piercing, narrowed. "Just don't make the mistake of taking Dare too lightly. Maybe he hasn't been the places you've been or done the things you might've done, but he's a hard man. He didn't get where he is with his forest lands reaching for miles by being timid. If he wanted something, he would be going after it, not wasting time with games."

The big hand fell on David's shoulder again. The voice was a low rasp, the burr of Scotland more pronounced. "Good luck, David Canfield."

David was given little time to ponder the red-haired Scot's enigmatic appraisal of Dare. There was information to be gleaned from the remark. Before he could think, he was in the wrestler's circle facing Dare. With a brief handshake and a curt nod, the match began. Hands locked, muscles strained, feet struggled for purchase. Body against body. Strength against strength. Skill against determination. Dare's grin flashed. David knew it was in sheer love of the game.

Time and again, they struggled. A stalemate unto exhaustion. Then error, miscalculation, advantage. David knew too late. He felt the crush of Dare's arms, the heat of his breath on his face. To the sound of a wild highlander's cry, David was slammed to the ground. The impact knocked the wind from his lungs and set the world spinning. As he lay on the ground, he heard the rustle of footsteps.

Breathing heavily, his magnificent body glistening with sweat, Dare looked down at David in stoic scrutiny. A grin broke over his face, and he dragged David to his feet. "Well done, Canfield." Rare praise, generously given. Bending, he picked up his shirt and slippers. When he straightened, he was abrupt. "Be at the Tartan Ball tonight."

"The program says by invitation."

"This is your invitation."

It had the ring of an order rather than invitation, but David said only, "Why?"

"Because Raven would like it." That said, Dare turned to leave the field.

"I won't wear a kilt," David called after him.

Dare turned back. "Maybe not this time, but you will. Next time."

"There won't be a next time."

"Won't there?"

"I'm leaving the valley in a few weeks."

"Then you're a bigger fool than I thought."

"I'm not a fool, McLachlan." The camaraderie born of combat faltered.

"Any man who walks away from Raven McCandless is a fool." Dare resumed his walk across the field, then dodged among tents erected by the clans and disappeared. David remained on the field. When he looked to the hillside, the crowd was breaking up. He searched for Raven among them. She was gone. He was alone, left to ponder the meaning of Patrick McCallum's remarks—and Dare's.

David stood in the shadows, listening. The music was a blend of old and new. There was the occasional piper's tune, but for the most part, the music was slow, rhythmic, instrumental. He'd had no intention in being here, meaning to leave as soon as he found Simon again. Instead, Jamie McLachlan found him—with an offer from Dare of a room for the night and a change of clothes for the ball. When he accepted, he told himself that it was only for the room, to give Simon and himself privacy and more time. But Simon was gone, flying back to Washington on a private jet, and David was lurking like a callow youth on the fringes of the festivities.

Raven was not hard to find. She was the center of a group that grew and shrank and shifted and changed. Only one thing remained constant. Raven. Her serenity was like a beacon. Every man, regardless of age, had managed to clasp her hand and kiss her cheek. When the music started Ross McLachlan, then Jamie, had led her to the floor. Patrick McCallum took her next. The big redhead held her much too closely, watched her too intently. David didn't doubt the Scot would have led her from the ballroom and into the night, keeping her until morning, if Raven agreed.

David shifted, at ease in his borrowed finery, but sickened by what he saw. It didn't matter that he told himself over and over again Raven was nothing to him. By the time Dare danced with her to a slow, sensuous tune, David was beyond telling himself anything.

Raven was a jewel in Dare's arms. She wore a slip of a dress so deeply red, it shone like the fire it emulated. Her hair was down, caught low at its curling ends with a matching rose of silk. The flower swayed at her back, drawing his eyes to the slender lines of her body. That body had been his once. Those lovely legs had wrapped about him, her arms had held him and all of Raven had been his.

Dare's head dipped to hers and lingered, as if he were whispering secrets. Then he laughed and spun her about, and Raven's gaze collided with David's.

Her cheeks were flushed, her eyes luminous. There was something magical about her. She was glittering stardust that would be gone with the rising sun. David had to touch her, hold her before the light took her. He stepped from obscurity onto the dance floor and muted incandescence flooded over him. The black of his clothing absorbed it. Only the band at his waist broke the somber lines. He seemed taller than his nearly six feet, and broader. His hair, a bit too long, gleamed against his collar. His features were craggy above the white ruffle of his shirt. If she was a flame, he was its shadow. As men were drawn to Raven, women found the man who moved among them irresistible. Their steps slowed, stopped, leaving their partners no other choice.

The chameleon of The Watch had never been so visible nor so oblivious. He knew only his need for Raven.

One by one, the revelers parted then turned as he passed them by. He moved with a dancer's step, slowly, prolonging the moment, keeping her forever in his eyes. In the heated throng, it was her fragrance that reached him first. Wildflowers. Until the day he died, he would remember wildflowers.

He had no idea when Dare moved aside, but Raven was in his arms and the music that had faded began again. Her clasp was warm at his shoulder and his nape; her body was cradled by his as she matched his steps. Her head was lifted, her face upturned. The arch of her throat was an invitation, the cleft of her breasts enticing, but it was her gaze, so dark, so deep, that held him. Their feet barely brushed the floor. Moving in concert, arms entwined, bodies touching, their eyes spoke what their voices did not. David's hands slid the length of her back, stopping at the swell of her hip. His palm rested there, his fingers splaying over the gentle curve. He felt the music in her body and answered with his. Their moves were mated, every step, every breath. He was lost in her. Every thought was Raven, every beat of his heart as he danced with her, feeling the music, never hearing it.

Raven's fingers tangled in his hair, stroked free of the disarray she created, then tangled again. Her touch was electric, her gaze hypnotic. Her lips were parted, her breath shallow, yet her breasts rose and fell in a gentle effort to be free of the scarlet silk. Beneath the silence, there was a waiting passion.

He wanted to draw her closer and with a kiss, set that passion free. He wanted to set it soaring and with it, his own. He wanted to feel her flesh against his and hear her whisper of delight. He wanted to fall with her into a languid sleep and wake again and again to take her.

He wanted. Dear God, he wanted. But all he could have was a memory... of Raven, who made him forget for a while.

The music slowed, faded. They stood, arms entwined, gaze unwavering. A sound intruded and David remembered. The dance was over. For a moment, his hands caught in her hair, then he was stepping back, his arms sliding slowly from her. Inch by inch, his fingertips glided over fiery silk, memorizing her body beneath it. Reluctantly, for memory wasn't enough, his hands fell away.

His chest rose in a deep, shuddering breath. With the back of his knuckles, he traced the line of her face. Raven's lashes fluttered and drifted down, but not before he saw the look of pain. The little distance between them became a chasm.

He waited, riveted to the floor. When her lashes lifted and her gaze rose again to his, he saw her courage and strength. He smiled, a bittersweet smile, and turned away.

Raven watched him weave through the crowd, the rose from her hair crushed in his hand. When he was only a half-seen shadow, the flash of scarlet was still visible. The music began again and Dare was there, taking her into his arms. With a look of regret, he slid a hand through her hair to draw her head to his shoulder.

David paced the lakeshore beneath the full moon. There was a secret chill beneath the sultry air, and leaves scattered and rustled with his step. Leaves of the poplar tree, the color of the sun, that fell in Indian summer. Golden harbingers of the autumn that was to come.

Soon, the wildflowers Raven loved would be gone. Beautiful flowers with ugly names. Rare flowers, hidden from his blind eyes until she taught him to see. He looked to her cabin, to the small light that shone there. How many things had she taught him? How much had he absorbed by being near her, from watching, from listening? In the few precious halcyon days they'd shared, how had she touched his life so profoundly?

As he'd sat in silence, watching as she brought flowers to life on stark canvas, and even as he struggled with his lust for her, something in Raven reached out to him. Something stronger than man's needs. Something he had never known and thought he never wanted to know. No one word could describe it, for it was many things in one. Peace, honor, contentment—and what frightened him most.

Love. What did he know of love? What did he want to know? "Nothing," he said aloud, and even he heard the falseness in it. Once, that was true. So true that he'd hated Helen Landon more than he was grateful to her for her misguided sacrifice.

Truth flashed through his brain like neon in rain. He hadn't hated Helen Landon. He hated his shame for not caring as she did. He hated his indifference, that he hadn't truly known her. He hated the grief that haunted the dark corridors of a mind already filled with ghosts.

Once, his answer was to hide his emotions deeply in his subconscious. Helen Landon couldn't be so firmly tucked away. He was more aware of her in death than in life. She marked him indelibly with the stain of guilt and stirred the ghosts he thought quieted. In his desperation, he had acted irrationally, choosing revenge in an effort to diminish remorse. Revenge that would have been tragic—but for Simon.

Simon, friend, mentor, had sent his reeling wounded agent to the one person he thought could help.

"Raven." David turned. The cabin's light still burned, as it had into the night, every night, since the Tartan Ball. Raven. Working through her troubles at her potter's table. Troubles he brought to her life.

How had she grown so wise? What pain lay beyond the serenity? What in her life had given her the strength and courage he'd seen on a shadowed dance floor?

Like a marauder, he'd come into her valley, taking her compassion, her kindness, even the gift of herself, and thrown them back in her face...an act of fear. Fear of feeling. Fear of caring for this woman when he hadn't for another. Yet he did feel and he did care. Never more than when she'd worn a dress of fire, her ebony eyes gentle on him. Every nerve had shrieked, and his heart had ached, and for the last time, he'd taken her in his arms. He'd wanted to dance forever, to hold her, keep her forever.

But the music had died and forever was done. When he let her go beneath the soft, shimmering lights, he'd seen himself mirrored in her eyes. A man who took and was incapable of giving in return. And Raven, a woman of towering strength and endless compassion, had understood.

In that moment, with the dancers about him, he'd seen the emptiness of his life and his future.

Now, suddenly, he couldn't face living the days left to him, unmoved and uncaring. The bleakness of it was more unbearable than the pain of caring. Because of Raven, the shackles and walls of a lifetime were tumbling, brick by brick, memory after memory. With some memories, he made his peace, with others, he could not. So he walked the shore, a man just beginning to understand, needing to sleep, but afraid of the dreams.

Once, they were only nightmares of a tormented subconscious, now, they were the purging of a soul. He dreaded the night, but he knew the dreams would make the healing complete.

Complete—and too late. The damage was done with Raven.

"I can still tell her that I'm sorry." Forgetting that bastards like David Canfield didn't apologize, he began to walk to the light.

Raven was at her table, working the clay, molding it. She was dressed in slacks and a shirt of some rough, woven material trimmed with a coarse lace. In her concentration, she was in a world apart, untouchable. Once, he would have believed that nothing had ever touched her, that the calm within her had never been challenged. Now he knew it was not true.

Stepping through the open doorway he stood beyond the circle of light waiting for her to sense his presence. Her sure, deft moves slowed; her nimble fingers grew quiet. Drawing her hands from the clay, still unformed and rough, she folded them in her lap. With the gathering of her strength and her guard in place, her gaze lifted to him. For a fleeting instant, David wondered what it would be like to have her look at him always, as she had the night he made love to her.

Nothing in his life had been for always. Nothing ever would be. Always. The word was ashes in his mouth.

Raven did not let him see her surprise. The dance at the Tartan Ball, with its desperate silence that neither could find the words to end, had been so final. It was his goodbye, and hers.

Yet, after weeks of coexisting with only rare glimpses of each other, David was here. He was tired, she could see it in his face. In the end, the valley hadn't been kind to him. With a twinge of regret, she wondered if she shouldn't have asked Simon to recall him after all.

For all his weariness, a feverishness burned in him, something that had drawn him to her. Quietly, for it was her way, she bided her time.

Abruptly, beginning in midthought, in a roughened voice, he said, "The terrible things you let me say to you. Never bothering to deny them."

"Would it have done any good to deny them?"

"I accused you of living an empty life, of being insular, selfish."

"It doesn't matter, David."

"You let me believe—"

"I let you believe what you wanted to believe."

"You could've told me."

Raven shook her head. "You were a stranger."

"I'm not a stranger now."

"What do you want to know?"

"How Raven McCandless came to be the woman she is."

Remembering how he had lain with her and loved with her, she wanted to tell him that he more than anyone knew who she was. Instead, she said, "I'm a woman, no more or less."

"It isn't that simple, Raven."

She sat, her spine erect, shoulders back. The slightest relenting would be her undoing. Silence ticked from one eternal second to the next. David folded his arms over his chest. A gesture that meant he would wait until she answered. "It's an ugly story."

"I've heard ugly stories before."

Raven sighed. She rarely spoke of her life. There was no secret in it. It was just too painful to put into words. Now, it was David who asked, and she couldn't deny him.

"McCandless is a respected name, but there was a time I didn't think I deserved it. A murderess shouldn't bear the name of those whose deaths she caused."

She braced for some expression of shock or disgust, but David's voice did not judge. "Your parents?"

"And my two younger brothers."

"You didn't kill your family, Raven." He said what he believed beyond a doubt.

"For a long time, I felt responsible. To a fourteen-year-old girl, it was all the same." She had turned away unable to face what she might see in his eyes. Now, as she risked a look, she saw he was standing as before, his face unreadable, waiting. There was no escape. He would hear the whole of it.

She didn't offer him a chair or waste effort on amenities that interested neither of them. Instead, she began to speak in a low voice, telling David things only Rhea McKinzie and Simon knew. "My father called himself a teacher. There were titles and degrees attached to his name, but Colin McCandless was husband, father and teacher, in that order. The degrees and titles were simply to make him better. Everything he did was to that end. His plan as father and teacher was to introduce his family to other cultures. We lived in Scotland, in France, in Austria and in other places. He taught in their universities. There was money. Not enough to be a burden or too little to be uncomfortable.

"That was the problem. Our lives were too ordered, our means too visible, their source too obscure. My father became suspect. A strange religious sect in a Middle Eastern country where we had settled, targeted him as a spy. Maybe he did small assignments for our government, or maybe he was exactly what he appeared to be. Whichever, he wouldn't have endangered us with anything serious."

"Any meddling is deadly serious to certain fanatical religions," David interposed.

That was a truth realized too late. Far too late. "We were going on holiday. My brother Douglas had chosen to go skiing for his tenth birthday. We were almost ready to leave for the airport when I remembered a book I wanted to read on the plane. They were waiting for me in the car when I came back from my room. Jamie, who was only two, danced in my mother's lap, calling for me to hurry. He wanted to see the snow.

"The sun was bright, as it was every day. As bright as mother's laughter. Douglas was trying so hard to be dignified. Dad reached for the ignition, and Jamie called me again. Except . . . except his tongue couldn't manage an *R*. He called me 'Waven' one last time, then everything stopped.''

"Jamie," David said softly, and Raven didn't need to be told that he'd made the connection between Jamie McLachlan and Jamie McCandless. If her brother had lived, they would've been of an age.

Raven had to move, leave the sound of her own voice behind. She wandered to the window. The night reflected her mood. Against a dark sky, ancient trees rose in black, jagged spires, the cavernous gloom beneath them as impenetrable as her soul had been.

She looked into the unchanging darkness. "When I woke, I was lying on my back. Flakes were drifting about me. For a moment, I thought we were already in Switzerland. It was hot. Too hot. My face hurt, and my back. I tried to get up and couldn't. I lay there in the snow. After a while, I realized it wasn't snow. Then I heard their screams.''

David's touch stopped her. As he turned her into his arms, she heard his voice, soothing, tender. Then he said no more, holding her until the pain passed. The stroke of his hand was peace in the storm. In another time, another place, she would've stood there forever. But it wasn't another time, or place, and after a while, she pulled away. With a wan smile, she turned again to the darkness beyond the cabin.

"When the bomb exploded, my father was thrown clear, but the rest of them—" She swallowed convulsively, then continued. "None of the doctors believed he could do it, but he waited for Simon. When he had Simon's promise to take care of me, he let go.'' Raven clutched at the lace on her sleeve, shredding it to confetti. "Then they were all gone. My mother, my brothers. My father."

"Simon brought you here, to his own mother."

"When I could travel. The burns, the concussion of the explosion, my guilt made it impossible for a while."

"Guilt, because you delayed the departure, because you weren't with them." David said the rest, sparing her that.

"Yes."

"Dying with them would've changed nothing, Raven." His conviction suggested a new understanding. "If they had a last thought, perhaps it was rejoicing that you weren't with them."

"I know that now, but it was a long time coming. The doctors wanted to put me in a hospital. Simon wouldn't hear of it. All I needed, he insisted was time and a good dose of Rhea McKinzie. They were reluctant, but he wouldn't take no for an answer." She smiled only with her mouth. Her eyes didn't change. "Nothing can sway Simon when he's certain he's right."

"We can both thank God for that."

As if she hadn't heard him, Raven began to speak of Simon's mother, Rhea. "She was already a very old woman, for Simon was a child of middle age. She was strong and so wise. With an iron will and infinite patience, she taught me that it wasn't wrong to survive when my family hadn't. That was the first step and the hardest. Then she taught me that love was a precious gift to be given unselfishly with no guilt attached. She made me understand that love given might not find an answer, but must be accepted and cherished as the treasure it is.

"You called it a burden, an unwanted sacrifice, a waste. Love is never a waste. I know that now, but for too long, I felt as you do. No one could get close to me. Despite Rhea's teaching, I wouldn't let them. For a while I left the mountains, trying to escape her truths, living awhile in a village in southern Arizona.''

Raven the innocent, who had loved no man until him. David ached to touch her in more than compassion, but knew he'd lost the right. "It doesn't snow in southern Arizona."

Raven wasn't surprised by his observation. David was kinder, more intuitive than he thought. He knew that each snowfall would, for a horrible moment, be ashes and the shriek of the mountain winds would be the cries of her family. "When Rhea fell ill, I came home. I realized then I could roam the world in search of peace and I would always fail, for these mountains are my peace. I haven't cried since I was fourteen, not even when I lost her, but I found my strength, if not my tears.''

"When it snows and the wind blows?"

"I cope. When I can't, there's Dare.''

"Alisdair McLachlan.'' Who, in Patrick McCallum's cryptic words, wouldn't waste time on a game if he truly wanted something. "Dare." *Who wouldn't waste time on games if he wanted Raven.* He was near when she needed him, and David was grateful. "A friend.''

"Only that. Always that.'' Glad for the change of subject, she said, "He regretted his behavior at the games. Out of sheer devilment, he wanted you to think there was something between us. When he realized he liked you, he wanted to make amends. The Tartan Ball was his way.''

"He didn't understand that it was too late for us."
Too many cruel things had been done; too many said.
Not even gentle Raven could forgive them.

"He understands now." *Dare understands that I love you,* she thought, *and that I won't try to keep you.*

"Raven, I didn't know."

For a crazy instant, she thought David had read her mind, then she realized he was speaking of her family. "There's no reason you should."

"I should have known you weren't as I tried to paint you. Hell." He ran a frustrated hand through his hair. "When I let myself be honest, I knew you were the fairest, least-selfish human being I've ever known." He'd come to apologize, but it was too late and not nearly enough. Instead, he could tell her that Simon had been right in sending him to her.

He wanted to turn her from the window so he could take her in his arms, but her grief had passed. He could touch her pain, but never again her joy.

"I'll be going from the valley soon. I think Simon will agree that my time here has served its purpose. I won't go empty-handed. I'll be taking the lessons I learned from you." Raven shook her head, but David stopped her denial. "I've learned that love is anger as well as joy. That it is its own punishment, its own reward. That it can be tears as well as laughter. True love expects nothing.

"Most of all, I've learned that those fortunate enough to love and be loved are blessed."

God help him, he would give his soul to hold her, giving himself to her, not just pretty words. His fingers curled into his palms. "I've learned more of the meaning of love by living here in the valley than I did in a lifetime beyond it." He touched her then, briefly, letting his fingers slide over her shoulder. Her head was bowed, the fall of her hair hiding the little he could've seen of her face. "Simon was a far wiser man than I knew."

Raven heard his footsteps taking him to the door. Before he left her, there was one more thing he should know. "David, love is forgiveness. Even when forgiveness isn't needed."

She heard his slow deep breath, could imagine his chest rising with it. Then after a moment, she knew she was alone.

Seven

"No!"

David bolted upright in his tumbled bed.

"No." Sliding his hands through his hair roughly, he tried to force the last vestige of his dream from his mind. He had dreamed little since coming to the valley. Now, in the week following the Tartan Ball, they'd become constant.

In the dark of night, when he succumbed to exhausted sleep, his life in The Watch poured from his subconscious, each dream a progression, each filled with destruction and the turmoil of greedy men. Each night, he walked amid squalor and starvation, unscathed, unable to help. He dreamed of betrayal, of a faceless woman. She called to him, but he didn't answer. She was hurting, and he didn't comfort her.

At last, he'd seen her face. Raven's face, with ash drifting over it like dirty snow. Raven, not Helen Landon. Raven, who had known tragedy and grown strong and serene.

Raven, who hadn't loved a man until—

He drew a cigarette from a tattered pack on the bedside table. A match scratched against the cover and exploded into flames. With a grimace, he bent to it and discovered his hand was shaking. When light from the match died, he leaned against the carved wood of the headboard, closing his eyelids. The fragile membrane was a shutter for the eye, but not the mind. With a will of its own, that wayward part of him turned to the woman who had been a flame in his arms.

In a room much like this, she had come to him, giving her greatest gift, herself. To him. Not to Dare McLachlan, who had been in her life nearly forever, who was there in her need. Not to the handsome, dashing Patrick McCallum, who would turn any woman's head, whose violate look made no secret that, were she willing, she would be his for a while. That was Patrick's way with women.

David felt a hot surge of anger at McCallum—for his lust, for the impermanence—then had the good grace to be ashamed. Like himself, Patrick was not of the valley. A man of the world, the big Scot had fallen under Raven's innocent spell. But Patrick hadn't tasted of her delights. He never would, for Raven would only give herself to the man she loved.

She loves me.

The words were a whisper in his mind. An echo of what he had known for so long. As with the wildflowers, he'd been blind until she taught him to see.

"She loves me."

And love is never a waste.

He was on his feet, spilling the covers from his bed. In his left hand, the forgotten cigarette. In his right, the rose she'd worn. He didn't recall taking it from the bedside table where it had lain every night since the Tartan Ball.

The flower nestled like a jewel against his flesh, recalling the touch of silken skin, the scent of wildflowers and silence. He remembered the mating of their steps, like the mating of their bodies. He remembered ebony eyes, luminous, gentle, holding his. But most of all, beneath the decorum, he remembered the waiting passion. Waiting for his touch, his kiss. Only his.

"Dear God! She loves me."

Love is forgiveness.

He was halfway to the door when he remembered that the rose was still in his hand and that he wore nothing. Another time, he would've laughed at the idea of calling naked on a lovely woman, but not tonight. Stubbing the unsmoked cigarette in an ashtray and laying the rose carefully in its accustomed spot, he scooped up his discarded khakis. He was too impatient to bother with belt or shirt or even shoes.

The clock in Simon's library struck the hour. Two o'clock, but she would be awake. Weaving his way through the familiar darkness, David stepped onto his porch.

Darkness. Unrelieved darkness. Her cabin was dark. For the first time in weeks, she wasn't working into the morning. God help him, her cabin was dark and not even the fickle moon would light his path to her.

A sense of helplessness swept over him. He wanted to go to her, to wake her. To make love to her. But he couldn't. For the first time in days, she was getting the sleep she needed. His hand came down with a crash on the rail.

"Fool!" His voice floated through the silvered night, and there was no one to deny him. She'd been waiting for him. Waiting for him to believe and to come to her. Looking at the darkened cabin, he knew he was right.

His heart contracted, and the blackness of night lay like a mournful omen about him. The windows of her cabin were empty, staring eyes. Unwelcoming. At last unwelcoming. Raven had waited until she thought the waiting was useless, and now it was too late.

He had closed the door between them many times, or had tried to. But Raven never had. She hadn't once shut herself away from him, until tonight. There was a finality about the darkened cabin that sent a shudder down his spine. He mourned the easy silences, the soothing comfort, the gentle elegance. They would never be his again.

God! What a slow-witted, slow-acting fool he'd been. Perhaps this, whatever it was, with Raven wouldn't have lasted. Perhaps they were too different for it to last for always. But he would have had today and tomorrow and the tomorrow after that. Instead, he had nothing.

Nothing.

Sickened, he stood poised at the steps, torn by the need to wake her. To ask for a little while. He wouldn't be greedy. She had given him so much. He wanted only a little, just for a little while. Then he would be gone from her life, a stronger man because of her, and she could love again.

He yearned to take that first step to her, but for the first time in his life, he understood what he would be asking.

As a night bird called and was answered by its mate, David turned to his own dark cabin. A splash at the lake stopped him. Hand on the door, head bowed, he waited. A night hunter? He heard the steady rhythm. For a time it ceased, and he thought, perhaps, he had imagined it.

Then again, the imperceptible splash. The lazy ripple of water. Raven. Swimming in her beloved lake.

Like a sleepwalker, he crossed the rough path. A soaring wind rustled the treetops. Skinny pines swayed and bowed. Over the mountain, too distant to be a danger, lightning flickered a promise of rain. On some level of consciousness, David was aware of it, of everything, but it didn't matter. Nothing mattered but Raven.

A stone clattered under his foot and Robbie rose from the underbrush, and at his side, Kate. Robert Burns, Raven's favorite poet. Katharine Hepburn, her favorite actress. Faithful guardians, keeping watch.

He couldn't see it, but he knew that both wagged their stubs of tails and flicked their ears. In his time here, they hadn't become playful with him as with their mistress, but because Raven accepted him, they had accepted him. And like her shadow, they were quiet, unobtrusive, ever present.

Beneath the hemlock, he waited, as he'd waited on his first journey into the valley. Kate came to him, snuffling at his hand until he scratched her ears. Next came Robbie, but standing aloof, never unbending enough to ask for affection. David smiled grimly. Were all males alike? Was it part of the masculine mystique to be above the need to be loved?

"Then we're fools, Robbie. Great, hulking fools." The dog shivered, struggled with himself but didn't relent.

Water lapped against the dock and David thought no more of Robbie or fools. It was time. She was near. He stepped from the protection of obscurity. The dock stretched before him. Putting one careful foot before the next, he paced its length. At the water's edge, eyes closed, he listened, not daring to watch. After a time, he opened his eyes and she was there, fingers grasping the edge of the dock, water surging from one last, glorious dive into the depths of the lake.

Golden eyes met ebony and held. As if he were watching himself from afar, David saw his hand reaching toward her, waiting uncertainly, hungrily, for hers. His heart stumbled beneath her dark, searching gaze. Then her grip relaxed on the rough boards and her hand was lifting to his, palm to palm, fingers clinging.

Amid a cascade of water, he lifted her from the lake. She was naked as he'd known she would be, and more lovely than he remembered. He didn't speak; he couldn't. He could only hold her to him, reveling in the swell of her breasts against his chest, the molding of her body to his.

"I hoped you would come." Her breath was sweet and warm against his shoulder, sending a lightning of its own through him.

"I thought I was too late." His whisper was roughened with fear.

"Never." She shook her head and was silent.

"Your cabin was dark."

"You could have come in the darkness to me."

"I did. The darkness of my own personal hell."

She drew away, unmindful of her nakedness, thinking only of David. There was a haggardness about him that suggested that he had, indeed, been through a private hell. But beneath it, there was a look, if not of peace, then its beginning. "And now, David?"

The night was a translucent veil, teasing, then revealing. She was magnificent, and his for the taking. But not until he wiped the look of concern from her face. He would see her smile as he drew her down to him. "It's done. I've made peace with the memory of Helen Landon at last.

"Love is a gift," he said, echoing Raven, not verbatim, but better, in his own words, making the thought more truly his. "Perhaps not to be returned in kind, but to be treasured." He touched her face, tracing the line of her cheek to her mouth, lingering there. "Simon knows magic." He kissed her, softly, slowly, with only his hand and his lips touching her. "Its name is Raven."

Raven trembled. "You really are all right?"

"More than I've ever been in my life." His voice was low, the roughness gone from it. "If it truly isn't too late."

Raven heard the strength and beneath it, the need. Turning her face into his hand, she kissed his palm. "Make love to me, David. Here by the lake where we first met."

"You're cold. You're trembling."

"Not from the cold, but still, you can warm me."

"Yes."

"Make the night more beautiful, David."

"The rain is coming."

"Not for a long time," she murmured, letting herself be drawn to him, knowing that his token resistance had been only that. A token. The prolonging of an exquisite need that would find an even more exquisite fulfillment. As their bodies met and her hands went to the snap at his waist, she murmured again, "Not for a long, long time."

When David woke, the night had changed. The moon that had been hidden behind the gathering clouds peeked through. Giving its blessing, it shone over them. The breeze that played among the treetops dipped now to the earth. It skimmed over their naked skin, turning their warmth to chill. Not even the reflected heat of Kate's black-furred body as she lay by David's side, or Robbie at Raven's, could deter it.

David looked down at the woman who slept in his arms. She was lovely. Her skin was tawny and golden against the vivid bath sheet beneath them. She was honor and goodness and magical peace amid a breathless, beautiful passion. He didn't understand how there could be peace as well as passion, would never understand. Like the tides of the sea and the moods of Raven's mountains, after the furor, there was tranquility, the time of holding her, of filling his mind and heart with the sight of her. Raven, with hair of midnight and spirit of sunlight, an exotic flower lying in guileless abandon against a field of blue.

He could watch her sleep forever, would wish this cherished interlude wouldn't end. Like the elusive stardust he'd imagined, it was not to be. Thunder, the passion of a mountain storm, rumbled, no longer in the distance. The threat of rain was reality.

Slipping his arm from her, he knelt over her, and gathering her again to him, rose to his feet. A massive Doberman rose on either side and walked with him the length of the dock. The rhythm of his step woke her. Drowsy, with her head against his shoulder and her lips brushing his skin, she asked regretfully, "So soon?"

"Only a change of scene."

"The rain."

"Yes, the rain," he answered, though there was no need. She was asleep again. At the dock's end, he paused and turned. It hadn't changed. Somehow, he'd thought it would. Ridiculous! As ridiculous and sophomoric as making love in the open on hard, splintered wood. Tomorrow, he would feel every one of his thirty-eight years in every muscle. But that was tomorrow. The night was not yet over, and making love to Raven was never ridiculous. Anywhere, anytime.

Anywhere. Anytime. Yet he chose his cabin. Not because it was closer or because the rain was imminent. In a way he couldn't explain, making love to her in *his* bed, just for the remainder of this one night, made her his as nothing else could.

It wouldn't last. He didn't expect it to. Neither did Raven. When she took his hand, by mutual and unspoken consent, they'd agreed to take what was given them, to treasure it for the little time they had.

Much, much later, when his need was quenched, if not sated, he sat by the bed, watching her sleep, memorizing the way her hair grew in a swirling pattern over her ear; how the corners of her mouth lifted in a sleepy smile; how the cleft of her breasts deepened as she tucked her arms about her. When she stirred and frowned at finding herself alone, he murmured softly, "I'm here, Raven."

When she reached for him, drawing him back to the bed, he knew a flicker of regret for the tiny seconds he'd wasted away from her. Then, when she rose above him, with her hair falling like a torrent of silk over him, there was no thought of anything but Raven.

* * *

Raven turned from her easel and looked into David's unwavering gaze. With a gesture that was not quite self-conscious, not quite comfortable, she asked, "What?"

"Nothing." David didn't smile, but his expression was calm, marked by contentment.

Though she'd come to expect his gaze on her and reveled in the softness she saw in this hard, brutal man, she had never grown accustomed to it. Could never take it for granted. He unsettled her. His look never failed to set her heart racing and her body throbbing. Her question had been simple reflex. A moment to gather her scattered wits. To rein in the desire a look or gesture could ignite.

Her life in the past three weeks, the last of David's sojourn in the valley, was a confusing mix of tumult and accord, of tenderness and brutal truths, of laughter and pain. The wildness in their coming together, utter sexuality, triggered by an uncalculated gesture, a look. The consuming desire that took her beyond thought or reason. The melding of bodies, joining in a fevered pitch, rising in a blaze that exploded in spangles of sunlight. Of love.

Each time, when she thought she couldn't bear it, couldn't live beyond it, the contentment came. And she discovered she lived, that her heart still beat in her chest, that only her soul had soared with his—when he was a part of her and she of him.

Because of the loving, it would always be so. No matter that he would be leaving soon, it would forever be so.

Survival, contentment, but never surfeit. Never that, for no matter how devastating and impossible, there was always the desire for more rippling barely beneath the surface. Rippling and surging, as now, with only a look from David. Perhaps such consuming hunger for a man's touch made her wicked or wanton, but Raven didn't care. These were days of enchantment. And if they never came again?

She wouldn't think of that. Tomorrow would come, but not yet. His eyes were on her, his book lying unopened on his lap. His body was taut beneath a surface negligence. Her own gaze swept him, languid with invitation.

"Nothing, David?" she murmured, letting her gaze dwell on the sudden rise of his chest as his breath caught.

"Only that I like to look at you," he said, so softly, she barely heard. There was pleasure in his tone, and more. "I've never known a woman as graceful or as lovely."

Raven's eloquent hands were quiet. Her head bent almost demurely as she had to look away from his tenderness. There was something he wanted to say, that he hadn't the words for, but her heart was nearly too full to keep still, her need too great to wait. Yet the tenderness from which her look had fled soothed her, drawing back her gaze like a flower to the sun. David *was* her sun.

"Raven." Her name was a caress. "You've given me the only peace I've ever known."

Raven smiled, and David saw her absolute serenity. He had always seen it, though he hadn't known how to value it. Now he knew of her loss, of her pain and guilt, and of the childhood horror that had robbed her of her tears. In the aftermath of tragedy, she found not bitterness and hate, but a gentleness and compassion.

She was serenity, but at a price.

He'd seen ugly things and had thought himself strong until he found Raven and discovered the real strength of survival is forgiveness. Forgiveness of oneself for surviving.

Peace. If she'd given him that, her job was done, her promise to Simon discharged. A man at peace with himself would become a whole man, sure, confident, rational again. If her love went with him from the valley? It was a gamble she'd taken and would never regret. Not one kiss or caress or even estrangement. Not when the look in his eye turned her blood to liquid fire that only he could cool.

Once, she hadn't believed peace and passion could abide together. Now, she knew that only a man at peace with himself and his world could give himself so completely. Her breath quickened. Her lashes fluttered to the sudden flush of her cheeks, then rose, revealing eyes filled with exquisite need. "Peace is sweeter... after."

Before she could finish her appeal, David was answering. His book fell in a heap on the floor. His chair clattered against the wall. As it overturned, he was across the room, sweeping Raven into his arms and striding down the hall. The carpet before the open door was a mighty temptation, but the look in her eyes promised repeated delights, and he wanted to surround himself with all that was Raven. The whole cabin was her. Every board, every fabric, but nowhere was it as vital as her bedroom.

It was her sanctuary, and no man but he had been there. He wanted to revel in the knowledge, to lie with her and let the scent of her drive him to madness. He wanted to tumble with her, skin caressing skin, and feel the crisp, sun-dried sheets at his back as flesh sought flesh.

Their time was growing short. But for this little time, they could forget.

From that moment, David stopped counting his time with Raven in days or even hours. It was as if he had a stopwatch in his head that could freeze a moment or a second. He was a thirsting man storing water for the drought, except his store was a heady wine too precious to measure.

During the long hours she was away at class, he busied himself in any way he could, always avoiding the clock. Because of the season, the days were growing shorter. She left in darkness and returned in darkness, making their time in the sun all the more precious. At day's end, always in her bed, always with her head pillowed on his shoulder, his last thoughts were of Raven.

Raven, dancing in a swirl of golden leaves. Raven, bending over a lowly dandelion he wouldn't have seen or thought beautiful, until she taught him what beauty was. Raven, who laughed now as if laughter was her breath. Raven, who teased him and banished his somber looks. Raven, who forbade him to brood. Raven. Always and everything, Raven.

"You've been quiet tonight," he said into the darkness over her bed.

"I know." She turned her cheek into his shoulder, her lips brushing his chest.

"Something wrong?" Tell me, he wanted to say. Tell me what dragon to slay, and I'll slay it. Or what right must be done, and I'll do it. But he didn't, for he was the dragon, he was the wrong. The wrong man, the wrong time, the wrong place. Nothing he could do would ever right it. Guilt, black and overwhelming, streaked through him. For pleasuring himself with her with such abandon. For taking the gift of herself and giving nothing in return. For allowing something as hopeless as it was wonderful to continue.

As if she sensed the sudden change in him and understood the blackness of his mood, she shifted, sliding her body over him. She wore the poet's shirt of rough, creamy cotton and frothy lace, his favorite. He liked the feel of her skin beneath it. Pearls beneath sand, satin under homespun, that teased him until, in a fever, he would draw it from her. But he didn't tonight. Her face was too solemn, her eyes too dark.

"Don't!" she demanded fiercely. "Don't spoil what we've had with regret. You were the first, but don't ever think that I didn't know what I was doing. I went into this with my eyes open. Don't scowl at me, and don't spoil the little time we have left with thinking this was wrong because it had no future. I learned long ago that not everything beautiful has a future."

"Raven." He tried to tell her that her first man should have been her last. The one and only love of her life. She was that kind of woman. It was what she deserved after the heartache of her youth. He wanted to tell her he was sorry he had robbed her of that. He needed her to understand that beautiful things could last—but not for him. He tried, but she shushed him with a kiss of such startling intensity, he fell silent at last.

"Don't even think that I would have been denied any of this. Not one moment. If there is a man out there somewhere for me someday, and if it matters that I loved you first, then I don't want him. And his wanting me would be a lie."

"No." Any man would want her, and he would never be a lie.

"Yes!" Planting her hands on either side of him, she lifted her body from his, affording a very enticing view of her breasts beneath her shirt. "There are times in our lives that make us what we become, or will become. If that man of the future does not love the woman you've made me, he won't love me at all."

"Then he'll be a fool," David said, and he knew he was speaking of himself.

"Yes," Raven agreed with such conviction that after a moment, she laughed. "If you take that as it sounded, you must think you've created a simpering idiot with a monstrous ego."

"I took it exactly as you meant it. You aren't an idiot, Raven. You're only kind and generous to a fault." When she protested, he shushed her by drawing her head to his chest, stroking the dark strands of her tangled hair from her face until she was quiet and relaxed against him. "All this began because I said you were quiet tonight. You never told me why."

"I wanted to ask a favor."

He felt the tension start again in her shoulders. He waited for her to continue, when she didn't, he said, "It must be pretty important if you're worried over it."

"I haven't worried as much as anticipated your answer."

"Is it something so serious?"

"I don't think so."

"But I will?"

"You will. You're going to say no in the mistaken idea that it's for my sake, for the protection of my reputation."

He was thoroughly puzzled, but one thing was true. He was concerned about her reputation. About what his stay in the valley had done to it. After the fiasco of the Highland Games, his solution was to stay out of public notice. His calls to Simon were made now at out-of-the-way phone booths. The few purchases he needed to make were never made in Madison. After the ball, he'd made certain he was never seen again with Raven. Perhaps it was too little, too late, but it salved his conscience at least a little.

"What is this favor?" He stroked her taut body. "I'll do anything, if I can."

"Jamie's recital. It's tomorrow in the college auditorium. Since the Highland Games, he admires you tremendously. It would mean a great deal to him, and to me, if you would come."

"No." David's body was suddenly as taut as Raven's. "Surely you realize that's impossible."

She pulled away from him. "It isn't, but suppose you tell me why you think it is."

"*This* is why!" he said almost angrily. "Anyone can take one look at us and know."

"They know already, David." She lifted her arms. The full sleeves of her shirt drifting from her wrists reflected the slanting light of the moon like glistening snow. The neck of her shirt dipped low over the fullness of her breasts. Its lace framed the lovely slope, slipping dangerously toward a darkened nipple that peeked through its coarse, loose weave. "What do you see?"

He saw a woman who knew the pleasure of love. A lovely, desirable woman. He wanted to lean forward and capture with his mouth the impudent nipple that played hide-and-seek with its shadowy veil of lace. As he felt the mounting desire that could sweep away even the blackest despair, he murmured hoarsely, "I see a beautiful woman."

Raven met his gaze levelly, refusing to give ground. "You see a wanton. A woman discovering the pleasures of an affair. It's obvious, isn't it? In the way I move, the way I speak, the look in my eyes. It consumes me and elates me."

"Yes," David admitted. Anything else would be a lie.

"Have you fooled yourself into thinking that my friends haven't seen the change? That they don't know what brought it about? Do you think that what's inside me switches off when I'm away from you? There's magic here." She rested the flat of her hand on the bed where she had lain with him so many times. "Magic that all the world can see."

"Why confirm what they only suspect? Let suspicions remain suspicions. It will be easier for you when I'm gone."

Anger flared; her face hardened. "I won't say I'm proud of this, David." Raven rose from the bed, facing him in the little light that found its way through the window. "But no one has made me feel ashamed. Until now. Until you."

She turned away, moving with an unnatural stiffness to the window, her shoulders hunched as if her world had turned sordid.

Suddenly, the room that was his world seemed too much. More than a bastard deserved. The bed, her bed, was cold and empty without her. He hadn't meant to hurt her or make ugly something she treasured. He only wanted to protect her from himself, from the harm he'd done. But wasn't it too late for that?

David remembered the Tartan Ball and the look in Dare's eyes as he stepped aside for David. Dare knew even then, the wise man that he was, that he couldn't protect Raven from some things.

David was on his feet, crossing the room to Raven as he had before, as he would again. At the window, he drew her lovely, unresisting form against his nakedness. In the poet's shirt, she was, indeed, a pearl beneath sand, satin under homespun. He would give anything to wipe the look of sadness from her face. Anything. But Raven wanted very little and for a moment, before he brushed the thought away, it rankled that it was so little.

"Raven." His voice was rough, unsteady. "Sweetheart. Smile and I'll go anywhere for you. Siberia or hell. Even Jamie's recital." She was so still, he had the sinking fear she wouldn't accept his clumsy entreaty. Had he made one more thing too ugly to survive. Then she was turning to him, promising him in a voice that trembled that Jamie's recital wouldn't be as cold as Siberia or as hot as his second choice. The look of disillusionment was not completely gone and her smile was tentative, but when her arms wound about his neck, he knew she was still his Raven.

He led her to her bed like a saddened child. Trying to reassure her, he tucked the flowing shirt chastely about her, and then the covers, before slipping in beside her. For the first time in his life, David Canfield understood completely how caring was more than passion, more than desire. In Raven's bed, he discovered there were untold pleasures in comforting a hurt, beautiful woman, and in holding her. Holding her until she finally slept.

Eight

The sound of voices lifted and soared as David stepped with Raven into the back of the auditorium. Madison was a small college, but its needs were handsomely met by an endowment made by a wealthy family. What was once their summer estate was now the college campus. On a misty summer morning, Great-great-great-grandfather Madison had found his bride among the locals. He never forgot or let his family forget. In their generosity, Madison provided amenities much larger colleges lacked. One was the concert hall that took David by surprise.

"Listen." He grasped Raven's arm, drawing her to a stop, forgetting the implications of this public appearance. "Listen to the sound. I'd wager a whisper can be heard in the back row as well as it is in the first."

"What the Madisons do, they do well." Raven continued to the aisle where three brawny men sat. The

McLachlans, as striking in contemporary dress as in kilts.

"Dare. Ross. Robert Bruce." David addressed them after each greeted Raven with a kiss. There was no time for more as the lights dimmed, signaling the recital was about to begin. David sat on Raven's right while Dare was on her left, with the younger McLachlans beyond. David hadn't the opportunity to assess the reaction to his presence. When the lights went out and Jamie strolled to center stage, he forgot to care.

The transformation was astounding. Imp had become virtuoso, distinguished in black tie and tails. Every move sure, every note perfect, Jamie's music was passionate and pastoral, powerful and subtle. Sounds that recalled rippling water and the crash of the sea. The whisper of the wind through tall pines, the majesty and solitude of the hills. Jamie played faultlessly, and when Raven's hand slid beneath his, David closed his eyes and listened. There were only he and Raven and Jamie's music.

Too soon, the recital was done, and the audience surged to its feet. There was an encore, and another, and a third, then Jamie, with a familiar rakish smile, begged off.

The crowd began to move to the doors. Ross and Robert Bruce excused themselves to speak with friends. Dare was engaged in conversation with a formidable dowager. As the hall grew quiet, David rose, with Raven at his side. He hadn't spoken since the lights had gone down. Now, he breathed a single word, "Jamie?" Then, "I'll be damned."

"You aren't sorry you came?"

David turned to find her gaze on him; her eyes were shining. He wondered if she'd watched him throughout the program as she did now. Anyone who saw her would have little doubt of her feelings, and David knew with a trill of pride that the look was for him. Lifting her hand to his mouth, he brushed a kiss to the back of her fingers. "I'm not sorry."

"David, Raven, if you can tear yourselves away, it's time. The reception's already begun." Dare's dark face was lit by a grin, a mix of pride and amusement.

"Is it?" David didn't look away from Raven.

"The custodian will be closing the hall shortly. No," Dare corrected as the lights went out. "The custodian *is* closing the hall."

"And Jamie's waiting." Keeping her hand in David's, Raven led the way from the auditorium.

The reception hall was small but done with the Madisons' style. As Raven was drawn into the crowd, David stepped back to watch. These were her friends, her people. How would they accept her now that her life included him?

"They don't care, David." Dare was at his side, a flute of champagne in each hand. "Those who matter are glad Raven has finally found someone."

"Am I that obvious?"

"That you're worrying about what will happen to her when you leave? Yes, my friend. You're that obvious."

"I have to go." David waited for a comment. When the man at his side made none, he continued. "I wouldn't fit in here. After a while, I would make her more unhappy by staying."

"Keep talking, maybe you'll convince yourself, if no one else."

David forced his attention from Raven, slender elegance in a tightly belted dress that drifted about her like amethyst smoke. Dare offered David a glass of champagne. His dark coat and light, ruffled shirt were much like the one he'd lent to David the night of the Tartan Ball. "Dare." David's grip on the flute threatened the fragile crystal. "Will you help her?"

"I'll be here, but there are some things I can't make easier for her."

"She's a strong woman. She'll forget me."

"Yeah. When pigs can fly and fools learn the word *can't* is a self-imposed limitation. You say you can't stay in the valley. Jamie says he can't leave." Dare broke off, watching his laughing, young brother, surrounded by a bevy of adoring girls. "Look at him. He's happiest when he plays, but hasn't the sense to know it."

"When he's older, he'll know where his happiness lies."

"As David Canfield does?"

Not even the gentleness of Dare's tone softened the scalding sarcasm. Before David could refute it, his arm was taken by a tall, thin woman with a mass of white hair caught in a chignon at the nape of her neck.

Ice blue eyes peering through a lorgnette impaled him. "So, this is the young man who's put the roses in our Raven's cheeks?" She was crisp, blunt, reminding David of his third grade teacher.

When Dare attempted an introduction, she cut him off with a regal gesture. "I know who Mr. Canfield is, and you can tell him who the old biddy is when she leaves."

"Old biddy, Dean Madison?" Dare dared not laugh.

"The old maid of the founding family, who didn't have the good sense to take what she wanted for the little time she could as Raven has." The lorgnette dropped to her bosom. Without its distortions, David saw her eyes were lovely. "I knew your scalawag of a boss, Mr.

Canfield. He was a student at Madison for a while. That Simon thinks highly enough of you to send you to his home speaks well of you. If you don't decide to rescind your resignation in your...ahh...former employment, come see me. Madison College could use a man of your experiences."

"As what, ma'am?"

"As an instructor, of course. Do you think I would waste your talents in criminology and diplomacy and skulduggery as a security guard?"

"My talents?" David smiled in spite of his efforts not to. "Are you so sure I have them?"

"Positive. Simon was your teacher, wasn't he?"

"Yes, ma'am."

"Checkmate. Dare," she addressed the man at David's side, "not one word to Jamie about *not* becoming a tree farmer. In fact, put him to work. So long that he can hardly find time to sit at the piano. So hard that when he does, all he can do is fall asleep."

"Give him what he wants," Dare said with a touch of irony.

"In spades. Mr. Canfield?"

"Dean Madison?"

"I'll be waiting." The regal back turned. They'd been instructed and dismissed.

"I feel like I did when Miss Halmer paddled my hand with a ruler in the third grade," David muttered.

"For me it was Miss Addison, fifth grade."

"Is she always like this?"

"Always."

"Lucky school. Lucky students."

"Yeah. You ready to brave the mob and give our compliments to my young genius?"

"Before you put his nose to the grindstone?"

"In spades."

"I liked your friends." The Corvette streaked over the road, its headlights brightening their path like day. David felt Raven's smile rather than saw it. "I know very little about music, except whether or not I like it. I think Jamie could make me like scales."

"He was pleased you came."

"Your Dean Madison offered me a job."

"She doesn't know."

David looked from the road. Raven was subdued, the gaiety he'd seen at he concert and reception dimmed. "What doesn't she know?"

"That this is your last week in the valley."

David slowed his speed. Leaving his left hand on the wheel, he slid his right hand into Raven's. She didn't move away, but beyond a smile, she didn't respond. The remainder of their journey was made in somber silence. It had begun. David felt it, the unconscious drawing away. The way of the mind and heart to soften a coming blow.

"I spoke with Simon today."

Raven looked up from her potter's table. She had recovered her composure after the concert and was again his tranquil companion by day, his passionate lover by night. In the evenings, she worked at her pottery.

"How is he?"

"He's well, but there's no break in the case. A lead, a phone number, hasn't gone anywhere."

Raven folded her hands in her lap. "How do you feel about the past now?"

David shook his head. Laying aside his book, he went to the window. "As if it all happened to someone else.

That Helen Landon died for a man who shouldn't exist anymore."

"Are you sure he does?"

"I'm not sure of anything."

Raven waited. She couldn't help him now. His choices must be his own, uninfluenced by anyone.

"There's more," he said, breaking the silence.

"Something that troubles you."

"Helen Landon's family has planned a memorial service. They've asked that I come."

"Where?"

"Tennessee."

"Will you go?"

"It's not very far away from the valley. A day's drive." He shrugged and fell silent.

Raven left the table, going to join him at the window. "It's hard facing people who've lost someone. Would you like me to go with you?"

"Would you?"

She touched him then, laying her hand on his shoulder. "Wherever you need me."

His hand clasped hers, drawing it to his lips, and she went into his arms. "Thank you," he murmured as they looked over the valley together.

"Young man." Her voice was as peremptory as Dean Madison's, but the wizened old lady with skin of wrinkled leather and thinning brown hair pulled into a punishing knot, bore little physical resemblance to her. She was perched on the edge of her wheelchair like a fledgling robin who might fly or tumble to the ground. "Come here."

David went to her, kneeling in the grass at her side. Raven felt a surge of pride as she watched him lean patiently over the old woman, listening as if she imparted the greatest knowledge. He had that talent. A way of giving his unwavering attention in an aura of grave interest, then, in a trice, of striking one breathless with a smile. When he relaxed and forgot, no woman was immune. Not even this one, who looked as impervious as shoe leather.

Raven moved nearer, over the grass of the cemetery, trod by Helen's departed mourners. She waited for the moment David would smile and this ancient woman of Tennessee fell under his spell.

"She was a wild one." Raven heard the old, quavery voice. "She did foolish things, then more foolish ones to cover them. She was slick. Not many saw her at it. But I did before they shipped me off to the home. I did, sitting in my corner, in my chair. She thought my mind was as dead as my legs, or she just didn't care that I saw her playacting."

"Children do that, Mrs. Landon. Your granddaughter was no different than other children in that."

"She was, Mr. Canfield. She was."

"Why did you decide to speak to me about this?" David asked, more to humor the lady than for any other motive.

"I sensed a sadness in you. Maybe our Helen caused it with her foolishness, maybe she didn't. There was a mystery in her death. In all the years I knew her, any mystery involving Helen was created by Helen." The old woman looked into David's eyes. "There's an investigation going on. Mr. McKinzie informed us of it today. Look into Helen's activities. Maybe your answer will be there, maybe not."

"You didn't like your granddaughter, did you?"

"I didn't like her scheming, but I loved her. That's why I don't want her to be the reason for hurt."

"Time's up, Mrs. Landon. Your son said to give you just five minutes with this gentleman, then to take you back to the convalescent center," said a brawny young man.

The old woman sent the nurse a withering look. "Convalescent! Humph! How do you convalesce from old age?"

Ignoring her mockery, the man in whites propelled chair and woman to a waiting van. On its side was a cheerful logo aimed at making growing old and infirm a joyful experience. As the lift raised the chair into the van, the dark eyes of the old woman never left David. Not until the doors were shut and the van moved away.

"You heard?" David asked as Simon joined them.

"It matched the version she told me."

"What do you make of it?"

"A crazy old lady who hated her granddaughter."

"Crazy like a fox." Raven spoke for the first time since the memorial service ended and the family gathered about David. She had bided her time, standing near but apart as they spoke to him in earnest tones, asking quiet questions with poignant need in their faces. Then, their goodbyes said to child and friend and sister, they'd gone. The last to leave was the old lady. "She loves her granddaughter."

"Honey—" Simon put an arm about Raven "—we can't investigate the ravings of every senile old woman."

"Not everyone, and not senile. Don't make the mistake Helen made. Don't assume her mind is as dead as her legs."

"You really think we should take her seriously?" This from David.

"What other leads do you have after all these months, Simon? David?" Raven waited as they got her point. Then, softly, "What other choice do you have?"

Simon addressed David. "What are your plans now?" His younger companions understood the unspoken—now that your exile is over.

"I'm going back to the valley with Raven for a few days. And you?"

"Back to Washington." Ruefully, Simon added, "To investigate our newest lead, as our lovely sleuth here suggests. In fact, my plane should have taken off ten minutes ago." After kissing Raven and brushing David's hand aside for a bear hug, he tossed them a jaunty wave, along with, "I'll be in touch."

Raven walked with David over the hillside to the Corvette. They were alone, removed from the bustle of the city below. Sunlight slanted through the trees, and crickets chirped in their rustling leaves. The air was so clear, it shimmered. The scent of woodsmoke whispered in the breeze. Colors were muted now, but soon, the sprawling forests would be dressed like gypsies.

Autumn, the beautiful end of summer. An ending, yet a season of riches. By drawing away from David, abandoning the best of times in fear of their ending, she had almost lost her autumn.

Almost. Her arm about his waist tightened, her step moved with his. She would remember this loveliness, how it surrounded her as she stood by the man she loved when he needed her. When he needed her, she thought, for a while.

"Raven. Thank you."

"It wasn't as difficult as you expected."

"Only because you were with me."

Raven stopped, linking her hands with David's. "There is an inn in a little glade along the way home. Even if she might have been as foolish or foolhardy as her grandmother thinks, I'd like to drink a toast to Helen there. No matter what else she did, she kept you safe." Raven's face was thoughtful. "We could be there by sunset."

"A toast to Helen," David agreed, "at sunset."

David's few days in the valley with Raven came and went, yet he showed no signs of leaving. Raven did not question it in the long, glorious days they spent together. Nor did she leave the valley. David did not make his expected journeys to one of a number of isolated phone booths, and for Raven, the daily trips into distant Madison ceased.

Though she'd worked at the college through fall registration and afterward, assisting the freshman class in orientation, her classes had ended until spring. These autumn and winter months she would devote to text and drawings for her book.

But in these special days with David, neither the book nor her drawings nor even her pottery could draw her from him. These were their halcyon days, days of happiness, of memories that must serve a lifetime. There was no looking ahead, no mourning for the time that was coming. Raven discovered that when one lived each day as if it were the only day, the day of reckoning did not exist.

This is paradise, David thought as he sat on the dock, a fishing pole wedged between the gaps of its planking. He glanced at the pole occasionally, not to see if a fish had taken his lure, but daring one to interrupt him. A cool breeze skimmed across his bare chest and ruffled his hair. He lifted his face to the sky, for once letting his attention wander from Raven.

He heard her laugh, and closing his eyes, let the sound drift with the wind over him. It was a lovely sound. The loveliest in the world. "David." He heard her voice and decided he was wrong. That was the loveliest sound, his name, with the laughter beneath it. "If I waited for you to catch our dinner," she continued, "we'd starve to death."

"No, we wouldn't. We could always make rock soup." He opened one eye and let the sight of her fill him. Other women might be dowdy in a tattered shirt and cutoffs that were even more disreputable, but not Raven. There was nothing that Raven wasn't pretty in, and turning it around, Raven was pretty in nothing. The illusion made him grin.

"You're thinking wicked thoughts, I can tell." She plucked a worm from the can beside her and made a show of nonchalance, but nothing hid the telltale flush that crept up her throat and over her cheeks. As she baited her hook and threw it again into the water, her lithe ease turned to clumsiness and the blush deepened. When David chuckled, she rounded on him. "What's so funny?"

"You are. I am. Everything." He looked at her, at the dock's edge. This was where he'd fallen under her spell. "I had forgotten." As he was likely to do of late, he spoke his thought aloud, and when she looked askance, he added, "I'd forgotten how to laugh. But now that I've remembered, it's addictive. The more I laugh, the more I want to."

"You've grown lazy, too," she retorted, but a teasing tenderness lurked beneath the words. "It's been so long since either of us has been out of the valley, our cupboards are nearly bare. It's fish tonight or nothing."

"You're forgetting rock soup." He had no fear of starvation. He knew from experience that beneath her magic hands and with the help of a well-stocked freezer and cellar, a little of this, a dab of that, a sprinkle of this herb and a leaf of another, she could produce an ambrosia worthy of the gods.

"What on earth is rock soup?" Reeling her line in, she inspected it and found a wily fish had managed to pick it clean while evading its barb.

"Didn't your mother tell you of the poor soul who had nothing but water and a rock for his soup until he enticed others to add their food to the pot for a share? At least, that's how I think the story went."

David chastised himself for mentioning her mother, for bringing painful memories into their perfect world. When Raven only laughed, saying her mother was an accomplished storyteller, but she seemed to have missed that one, he relaxed, if only a little. He was reminded of something he needed to speak of to Raven, an issue that weighed on his mind, one he'd skirted for days.

Sitting as he was, his head resting against a weathered post, he watched her cast and reel and cast again. She was an expert, putting the line exactly where she wished. Only, the fish were not cooperating today. The muscles in her arms flexed, then tensed with the drag of the line. With a shake of her head, she began to reel in again.

She was a far cry from the spinsterish thirty-year-old he'd once envisioned. Even farther from anything he'd branded her. But for the spill of her loosely bound hair and the sway of her breasts beneath the shirt, she could have been a young boy. A lissome athlete whose every move was unstudied vitality. Except today. Today, there was an inner quietude, a thoughtfulness ever present within the teasing and the banter.

Her line bobbed and pulled taut for an instant, then went slack again. Raven reeled it in, secured the reel and hook and put them away. "The fish have something on their minds other than feeding. As you suddenly do." Hands on hips, she surveyed the man whose smile had faded.

"Raven, there's something we need to talk about."

"Yes, I think there is," Raven agreed, and when he offered his hand, she took it, letting him draw her down beside him on the dock. Sitting with her hand still in his, she waited for him to speak.

"When I first came to the valley, I did a lot of thoughtless things. I was careless, criminally so." With his thumb, he stroked the tender flesh of her wrist, feeling his pulse joining with hers. "I've made mistakes in the past, and borne the consequences. But this time, there's more than myself to consider."

Raven stirred, started to speak, then subsided. He needed to say what he felt he must.

"We have loved well, but not always wisely." He faltered, his mind on the times that the sweep of passion overwhelmed them. When wisdom was forgotten. "There were times when you weren't protected."

"But not many," Raven offered quietly. When David had discovered she was inexperienced, he had discreetly assumed the responsibility of her protection. And, yes, there were those times when neither considered it.

"One thoughtless act could be enough. You've helped me put my life back together. The price mustn't be your own."

What would you do, David, if our passion were fruitful? Would you stay in the valley? Would you stay with your child and me? The question trembled on the tip of her tongue. She wanted desperately to know. Did such answers matter when his concern was unfounded? "We weren't always wise," she said in a low voice. "But there's no baby, David." She looked to the horizon. "I'm not carrying your child."

Instead of satisfaction at having his intuitions confirmed, David felt a moment of piercing disappointment. Disappointment turned to anger. Anger became loathing. He hadn't the right to wish that this lovely woman, who had given her love, would give life, as well.

"I thought not," he said at last. "But I had to be sure."

"There's nothing to keep you in the valley."

"No." He waited for the elation, the joy of freedom. This was what he wanted. Wasn't it?

Drawing Raven into his arms, his cheek resting against her hair, he stared blindly at the horizon and wondered at his sense of loss.

The telephone jangled in the darkening twilight. David's hand went immediately to the receiver, lifting it from its cradle to keep the phone from ringing a second time and waking Raven. Though he was completely alert, it took him an instant to comprehend the message delivered in a hurried, broken voice. In shocked tones, he murmured assurance and his thanks.

He replaced the receiver gently, but when he turned to Raven, he found her watching him.

"What's wrong?" Their lovemaking that had filled the late afternoon and the sleep that followed were forgotten in her concern.

He didn't have time to cushion the blow, so he said what he must abruptly, "That was Simon. There's been a break in the case. He's been shot."

Raven's hand flew to her throat. There was not enough air to breathe. "Is he..."

"He'll live," David said tersely. "Thank God the bastard who shot him doesn't know that. He does know where I am, Raven."

"Now he's coming after you," she whispered. "He has to before you find the same clues Simon did."

"Us. He's coming after us. He's traced me to the valley and you."

"Then what can we do?"

"Simon was ambushed and left for dead. He was unconscious for hours. His assailant has that much time on us. He could be anywhere."

"He could be here already," Raven said. "Watching us."

"Or the road."

"Do we stay here or do we go?"

"We go."

"If he's watching the road, we'll take the trails." She wasted no more time with questions. Sliding from the bed, she threw off the poet's shirt and slipped into jeans, a heavy shirt and boots. David was only a button or two behind her when she straightened, saying, "I'll pack what food we might need for a few days on the trail. You see to the rest."

David allowed himself a moment to watch and admire her single-minded purpose, the economy of motion, then turned to his own tasks.

Nine

***

Darkness would be their shield. Until they left, David told Raven, they would keep their usual schedule. Moving carefully through their preparations, they avoided being silhouetted against the windows, yet to any watcher, displayed no undue caution. They laughed and talked as on any night. Only David heard the disquiet in Raven's voice.

She went to the door, opening it only a little, looking for her dogs. They were not in their accustomed place. Perhaps they were off on a rare foray into the forests. Whatever the cause of their unusual absence, Raven refused to let her worry distract her.

David felt sympathy and admiration for her. She loved the massive Dobermans as much as she loved any human, but she faced this new trouble with the courage he'd come to expect. She went once more to the

door. His heart lurched in regret as she closed it fu-
tilely. She was pale as she resumed her packing.

As he checked off their supplies against a mental list,
David was pleased by her grasp of the situation. Her
understanding of their needs. She'd gathered dried
fruits from her cellar; they needed no preparation, and
were light to carry. There were canned goods and water
and a bedroll. Their departure could be as simple as
walking out of the valley to safety, or they could be cut
off completely, left to rely on trails in a lethal game of
hide-and-seek. The trip over the mountain would take
days. Raven planned for every possibility.

David regretted that their only weapons were as-
sorted knives gathered from her kitchen and a rifle she
kept for emergency use. With his service revolver, a
powerful weapon that was never beyond his reach, their
armament was little enough but would have to serve.

"Raven," David called when he was certain nothing
remained to be done. She looked up from braiding her
hair. "It's time."

Raven nodded and went to her bedroom, where she
turned on the lamp by her bed. She waited there while
David saw to the doors and extinguished the lights in the
rest of the cabin. Then he joined her in the bedroom.
Together, they waited the time normally needed in pre-
paring for bed. At last, David nodded, and Raven
turned out the lamp.

"This is it." In the darkness, he sensed her drawing
near. He didn't ask if she was frightened. Only an idiot
wouldn't be frightened when faced by a stalking killer.
Her hand on his arm, steady, lingering briefly, signaled
she was ready.

Moving like a cat, with Raven in his wake, David left
the bedroom and crossed to the front door. He hesi-

tated. "This may be a fool's exercise. There might be no one out there."

"He's there," Raven answered in a calm voice. "Or if not, he will be. He can't risk your finding the same clues Simon has. When he realizes he hasn't taken you by surprise, he'll suspect Simon survived and revealed his identity."

"Jeter," David said, giving a name to a faceless enemy. "His name is Thomas Jeter."

"Then we must act on the assumption that Jeter is out there waiting for you. For us."

David was so still, so silent, Raven wondered what thoughts were weighing on his mind. She waited patiently, giving him space. After a time, she touched his shoulder. "David?"

"I know." He covered her hand with his. The heat of it warmed the cold coil of dread. "I know," he whispered. "But first, this."

One hand slid about her waist, the other cupped the back of her head. His lips were on hers, tenderly but with a building hunger. There was an urgency in his kiss and in the intimate caress of his tongue. His arms were steel about her, melding the softness of her curves to the hard planes of his body. Clutching fingers drove into her flesh and were like a vise against her skull. Hunger and need and fear for her were in the devouring kiss. He was as desperate as he'd ever been. He wanted to draw her closer, to keep her safe at any cost.

When he drew away, his hands framed her face. "Promise me that whatever happens, you'll stay out of harm's way." Memories of another woman, of another place and of foolish sacrifices rushed in a tide of horror through his mind. "Promise me."

Raven understood his apprehension. As much as she could without a blatant lie, she promised, "I won't do anything foolish."

He held her a moment longer. Sighing, he released her. "I'll have to settle for that."

Raven bent, shouldering her small bag of supplies. David touched her face one more time and felt the brush of her lips as she turned her mouth into his palm. He had to struggle against the need to draw her back to him simply to hold her. A breath shuddered through him, shattering the silence that had fallen. His hand fell away from her face, his fingers flexing into fists. Enough time had been wasted. Too much. Abruptly, David signaled it was time to go.

Words were no longer necessary, and neither spoke again. David opened the door only enough to slip through. He moved in a crouching run to the railing at the side of the porch. As Raven slid beneath the rail, only a fraction behind David, she was thankful she'd changed into sneakers rather than the hiking boots. Boots would have been sturdier for the climb, but when quiet was of the utmost importance sneakers were better.

She followed David across the yard, praying that the dogs wouldn't choose this time to return and give them away. She realized by the path he was taking he intended to travel in a wide circle, merging with the road at a point beyond danger.

Despite the hint of chill in the air, sweat poured down her face and into her eyes. A spot between her shoulders prickled and burned, waiting for the slamming force of a bullet. Running a pace behind David, she wondered if this was how his life had always been, waiting for the bullet that had his name on it.

At the forest's edge, under its black canopy, David straightened. By his soft sigh of relief, Raven knew he'd been dreadfully worried by this mad dash over open ground. Allowing her a second to catch her breath, he began the circle that would lead to the road.

"No." She caught his arm. "This way."

"We'll try the road first. The supplies were just in case—"

"We aren't going to the road. We aren't going to try."

"Raven, I have to get you to safety."

"Until Jeter's stopped, there is no safety for me." Before he could argue, she stated the obvious. "You've said he'll know Simon warned you. The next and obvious deduction is that I know, as well. Neither of us will be safe again, David. Not until Jeter is caught."

"I have to get you out of here," David said doggedly.

"And risk losing him?"

"That doesn't matter."

Raven felt a lift of pleasure. She concerned him more than the revenge he'd wanted. David had never said he loved her, but she wondered, hoped that he did—at least a little. But that was to be savored another time. The issue now was life or death. "It matters to both of us. We have to stay in the valley and draw him out. To end this once and for all. If we don't, neither of us will have any peace again. I don't want to live my life looking over my shoulder."

"Raven, we haven't the time to discuss this."

"He'll come after me, David. So why not use me as a decoy?"

"No!" He grasped her arms, his fingers digging into her. "Dammit, Raven, I've already been responsible for losing one life to this man. I won't be for another. I won't lose you. I can't!''

"You won't," she said, wondering if he understood what he was saying. Aware of it or not, he was saying that he loved her. "There's a ridge on the mountain. From there, we can see and be seen. Yet it will be easily defended. I only intend to let him catch a glimpse of me. To draw him to it. The rest will be up to you."

"And if I fail?" he asked bleakly.

"You won't fail. We have too much at stake." It was the only way. He had to see that. He couldn't let Thomas Jeter slip away. For their safety. For Simon's.

"All right," he agreed at last. "We'll go to your ridge, but at the first sign of trouble, you're leaving."

"Alone?"

"Yes. Alone."

"We'll circle this part of the lake," she said quickly. Then, before he could demand another promise she wouldn't keep, she answered, "I'll lead."

David fell into step behind her. She knew these mountains better than he, and from the equipment she possessed, he knew she'd camped in them.

A quarter of the way around the lake, they began the ascent. They climbed steadily for two hours. David guessed that by day, without hampered vision, it could've been done in half the time. Near the crest of a ridge, trees began to thin, then disappeared. Raven led him to a natural meadow that was tiny and grassy and strewed with granite.

"This should do," she said, laying down her pack as she faced the valley.

David joined her at the precipice. She was right. Their view of the valley was unobstructed. As was the valley's view of the ridge. For the first time, he thought her plan would work. If he could get Raven away, it would be perfect. The mountain at their back was rugged, but she was expert enough to take herself over it and down, out of danger.

"No." Her voice was low and firm. "I know what you're thinking. I'm not going, David. We're in this together."

"I can handle Jeter better if I don't have you to worry about."

"That won't work. I'm here to stay. You won't be able to draw him out if I'm not."

David felt his temper rise at her stubbornness. "Since you have all the answers, would you care to enlighten me?"

Raven's own temper flared, but this was the time for cold logic, not fiery encounters. Giving herself time to cool down, she went to her pack and unzipped it. From it, she drew a can and a belt. With an object in each hand, she said, "I'm going to bring him to us with a careless mistake. One you wouldn't make. He'd suspect a trap, if you were alone, but with a clumsy novice, he wouldn't."

"I'm listening."

But not convinced, Raven knew. "The morning sun will strike this mountain full force by seven. Any bright object will catch its rays."

"The flash will be seen in the valley," David mused.

"A carelessness Jeter wouldn't believe for a moment from you." Raven was repeating herself, but she had her point to make. "One glimpse of me and he'll think he's found you, that he has you because of my stupidity."

She was right about the sun. Grudgingly, David admitted it. "It might work."

"If it doesn't, there's another probability."

"Robbie and Kate."

"They'll find me." Then almost under her breath, she added, "If they're able."

David went to her, sinking with her to the grass. He wrapped his arms about her, murmuring into her hair, "They will be able, Raven. Jeter isn't the prissy, clumsy fool we thought, but I doubt he's the sort who could take on two Doberman pinschers."

"If they're alive, they'll find me."

"Leading Jeter straight to us. That's more his style, to watch and follow."

Raven didn't believe a word, and neither did David, but it was something to hold onto. A comforting fantasy to keep her mind from the other alternative. Pretending her dogs were alive and well, she left him to begin setting up their fireless camp. When David recalled his experience with the rattler on a shelf of granite, she agreed the boulders would provide good cover in the light of day, admitting she preferred the open meadow by night.

Since this was to be a cold camp and neither was hungry, she finished quickly. The last thing to do was to set the guard. David insisted that he take the entire watch. Raven refused.

"Dammit, Raven," he exploded. "I didn't say I didn't trust you to do this. I said you needn't do it."

"I say that I do, and I *will*." She was unperturbed by his exasperation. "Contrary to what you want to believe, you need the rest more than I. Our lives may rest on the speed of your reflexes. Even David Canfield, man of iron, must understand that. Take the first watch. I'll relieve you in three hours."

As she walked away to her bed roll, David felt an urge to laugh. He'd been bested with admirable ease. He didn't doubt she could do as she said, and do it well. He watched as she settled into her bedroll and turned on her side. In a moment, her breathing grew shallow and easy. Her lashes lay like shadows against her cheek. Her single braid fell over her breast. David wondered if her sleep was genuine or feigned.

"You're quite a woman, Raven McCandless," he murmured, and took up his watch.

"David." He was shaken awake. He hadn't intended to sleep at the end of his watch. Glancing at the risen sun, he realized he had. Raven crouched beside him. "He's here."

Flinging back his covering, David went to the precipice. Below a man was moving cautiously over the valley floor. "Jeter! And you can bet your last dollar he's armed."

David whirled about. Raven's can was already set on a misshapen jut of stone. The label had been peeled from it. Shadows cast by the morning sun were slowly shrinking away from it. In a matter of minutes, it would glitter in the autumn morning. He turned to Raven, studying the serviceable shirt, the heavy jeans, the bright, buckled belt that flashed and dimmed with every sunlit move. A beacon, summoning Jeter.

David's heart was suddenly pounding, his chest throbbed with its force. The sound of a rising wind and the call of a jay were lost in the thunder of his heartbeat. Fear churned in his gut. Not for himself, but for her. "Take off the belt, Raven."

Her lips moved, but the sound was swept away by the wind. "For God's sake, Raven, take off the damn belt. For all we know, Jeter could be a sharpshooter, a sniper.

All it would take would be one bullet." His chest heaved. His eyes closed. "Take off the belt . . . please."

Raven was startled by his intensity. Then slowly, her fingers moved to the buckle and the belt fell to the ground. David stared down at it, watching it wink in the sun. When he looked at her, she saw relief in his eyes. Relief and something that made her spirit soar.

"You've done your share." David's tone was strained. "Now take cover. It's unlikely Jeter will be here before nightfall. Just in case, I want you out of the line of fire."

Raven didn't argue. He needed total concentration. All his senses must be attuned to Jeter. "You'll let me know if you see any sign of Robbie and Kate?"

He nodded but didn't answer. His face was bleak, and Raven knew then that he thought the dogs were dead. Perhaps they were. They'd never strayed this long before. But she couldn't believe they weren't coming back. She had to hope they were still alive.

She moved to obey, the forlorn slope of her shoulders tearing at him. As she climbed a small, grassy incline, he called after her. "If this doesn't work, get out. Take the roughest trail and don't look back. Jeter won't know these mountains like you do. Promise me you won't waste time here."

She stiffened, listening, her back ramrod straight. When he fell silent, she shuddered, her body bending forward as if she'd been struck. As quickly as it had come, the weakening was gone. Her voice was low but steady. "I won't look back."

She threaded her way through the scattered granite to a fortresslike formation of stone and hillock, then disappeared. The meadow was empty. David was alone.

He moved to the edge of the precipice, his thoughts solely on the man who prowled the valley floor.

Raven knelt by David in the twilight. She'd stayed out of sight in the long, anguished hours of watching, leaving her position only to bring David food and water from their meager supplies. She offered water now. He took the cup, his fingers brushing hers, and drank. It was warm and metallic, but quenched his thirst.

"Anything?" she murmured as she took back the cup.

"Nothing for hours."

"Do you think he knows we're here?"

"He knows, Raven. He was smart enough to bury himself under Simon's nose. He's smart enough to find us. It's just a matter of time." David touched her cheek, wondering if he would ever hold her in his arms again.

Raven's hand closed over his wrist. Her lips touched the taut flesh at her fingertips. She smiled, a little wistfully, and stood. David heard her footsteps whispering through the drying autumn grass, but he kept his attention on the valley and the trails leading to their mountain refuge.

"Robbie!"

He heard her cry and spun from the long slab of granite that served as his post. Every instinct jarred with a sudden sense of wrong and danger. "Raven! Don't!"

His warning came too late. She was racing heedlessly over the meadow toward the black dog that half crawled, half stumbled toward her.

"Raven!" David called again, but too late. Even as he spoke, a shadow materialized from the underbrush. Arms closed about her like a vise. A Jeter that David had never seen whirled to face him. The gun in his hand was pointed directly at Raven's head.

Blood drenched the shoulders of Jeter's shirt and ran in crimson rivulet's down corded arms. Robbie's blood, not Jeter's. He'd carried the wounded dog up the mountain beyond them and then down. A certain lure to draw Raven into his grasp. David felt bitter respect for the cunning mind and brute strength needed to execute it.

Raven was pale and taut and silent. A gory sleeve crushed her back against Jeter. Her throat was smeared with Robbie's blood.

Jeter grinned and motioned for David to drop his gun. A haze of rage as red as blood screamed in David's brain. Like a savage, he wanted to streak across the clearing to rip the offending arm from Raven. He wanted to destroy the man who dared to touch her, violating her goodness with his treachery. A taunting smirk told him Jeter wanted it, too. The man wanted to gun David down in that wild, mad rush.

Then, what chance would Raven have? David's fingers opened. The revolver fell at his feet. Deliberately, he blanked Raven from his mind, focusing his attention on Jeter. The man had gotten to the clearing, close enough for a shot, two shots, and he hadn't taken them. The little bantam wanted to strut. He wanted his moment of glory. He meant to gloat before he did what he'd come for. David hoped to turn that need into a chance for Raven.

Forcing himself to relax, David measured his opponent. Jeter was built like a small tank. The powerful, compact body had been concealed for years by skillfully fashioned suits. A sardonic smile tilted the grim slash of David's mouth. "My compliments to your tailor."

"He had his uses." Jeter dismissed the reference to the strength he'd kept hidden.

"Had?"

"Past tense. Like your beloved Scot."

The arrogant bastard thought he'd beaten Simon. It was a slim chance, but it was the only one David had. His laugh taunted. "It takes more than a cheap traitor to do in an old fox like Simon McKinzie."

"Don't waste your breath. I saw him."

"Simon might have been down, but he wasn't out. Who do you think warned us? Who knew where I was but Simon?"

"Anybody could've found out. I did, by tracing this little lady's call to Simon. She was with you at the services for that simpering fool, Helen Landon."

"Who was looking for me, Jeter? Except the man who must be sure his link to Helen Landon was never discovered?" A vague motion caught at the edge of David's peripheral vision. Not Jeter, whose gestures were dramatic and calculated, nor Raven, inanimate and mute. Something moved beyond them, but David couldn't risk a look. "Simon got too close for comfort, didn't he? And you couldn't be sure how much I knew. You had to get both of us." He let a jeer creep into his words. "Except you failed with Simon."

"You lie!" Jeter's voice took on an edge of uncertainty.

"Do I?" There was movement beyond Jeter again, the sway of grass, a shivering shadow.

"Enough!" Jeter's voice slashed through the meadow. "I'm tired of this little game. Move to the ledge, Canfield."

David hesitated. Jeter jerked Raven's head back by her braid, jamming the barrel of his gun viciously into the soft curve of her chin. In the failing light, David saw a thin trickle of blood at the corner of her mouth.

Jeter's eyes never wavered. "Move."

"No, David!" Raven's cry was garbled from the brutal pressure.

Another blow like the last could easily crush her throat. He had no choice. Stepping closer to the ledge, he ignored the yawning chasm below. "It was you all along. You used Helen, didn't you?"

"This discussion's over. You're first over the ledge. After a while, the little lady will join you." Jeter clucked his tongue in mock remorse. "Climbing accidents are so sad."

"Simon will know better."

"Simon's dead!"

"Then who warned me?"

"Shut up!" Jeter was cracking. Pulling Raven roughly against him, he used her braid to bend her head at an impossible angle. Her strangled moan had David whirling from the precipice. He didn't care what Jeter did to him. It didn't matter, so long as he bought time for Raven. He felt the ricochet of a bullet and heard Raven call his name in anguish. He braced to attack as a bolt of black lightning streaked from the underbrush.

One hundred twenty pounds of snarling fury drove Jeter to the ground. He lost his hold on Raven. As he clawed at her, Robbie's glistening fangs closed like a steel trap, shattering his wrist. Jeter shrieked and struggled to turn the gun on the wounded dog as David kicked it out of his hand.

Like a mad thing, Jeter flailed at the dog. "Robbie!" Raven's command cut through the frenzy. No more was needed. The battle was done. Robbie backed off, limping to his mistress with the last of his strength.

David spared a glance for Raven, assuring himself she was unharmed. She was down and there was blood on her—Robbie's blood. With a grateful heart, David bent to deal with the fallen Jeter.

The moon was rising in a black sky still streaked with the fading fire of the sun. That beautiful aura, when day met night, held no magic for David as he crossed to Raven. She was a grave image in the pale darkness, only her hand moved lovingly over Robbie's still body. Moisture-laden grass cushioned the sound of his steps, yet he knew Raven heard. She heard, but still, he called her name. Only her name.

"Raven."

When she looked up at him, smiling a sad smile, he crouched by the great dog, his hand like hers stroking the heavy fur. After a time, she leaned her cheek to the sleek, dark head cradled in her lap. Robbie stirred and licked her hand. The meadow was hushed, even the wind was still. When she straightened, her eyes were dry.

"He's gone," she murmured, and David heard the grief locked inside her.

"Yes." But Robbie would never be truly gone as long as Raven lived. David looked out over the valley, remembering the bitter man he'd been. Understanding at last the man he'd become. He thought of the past and of Helen Landon, and felt neither anger nor guilt. Whatever Helen had done, for whatever reason, she'd been instrumental in bringing him to Raven.

And here on this hillside, in the name of love, he would've done what was needed to protect this magnificent woman and asked nothing in return.

When the night grew chill in the higher altitude, he rose. After seeing to Jeter, who was trussed uncomfortably like a mummy, he built a fire and brewed the sweet, dark chocolate Raven had packed. When it was done, he took it to her. She wouldn't drink it, but the heated cup could warm her hands.

Sitting beside her, he drew her back, into his arms. Her sigh—soft, weary, yielding—told him all she hadn't said. With his lips against her hair, he held her and dared to dream of a future. Tomorrow, he would take Jeter down. Then Robbie and Raven.

He would be needed in Washington for a while, but when he was free again, he would come back to the valley.

Ten

"**H**ave you heard from Raven?"

David shook his head, avoiding Simon's probing stare. He moved to the window that overlooked hospital grounds. Simon would be here for a few more weeks of therapy, then he would be going to the valley to convalesce. David had been assured by harassed doctor after harassed doctor that, though Simon's recovery was slow, it would be complete.

Now David shrugged his shoulders with a nonchalance that fooled exactly no one. "I haven't heard from Raven since she was in Washington to see you."

"Then why are you wasting time here?" Simon growled. "Jeter's put away. We know what he was and for whom. I have the solemn oath of the government involved that his contacts will be, shall we say... removed. He was small potatoes. Wheeling and dealing in penny-ante stuff. A disgruntled, self-important government official looking for a quick buck and a little glory as he climbed the ladder to power.''

''Helen Landon paid for his ambition.'' David hit the window with a force that threatened it. ''He destroyed her, with my help.''

''Your conscience should be clear about Helen. She was exactly what her grandmother said, a foolish manipulator who got in over her head.'' A sad frown flitted over Simon's face. ''She was my mistake.''

''How do you figure that?'' David faced Simon again, the tensions of the city, The Watch, his old life were there again in his eyes.

''Poor judgment. Poor screening. Some of her outstanding qualifications blinded me to important flaws. Flaws that outweighed any qualities.'' Simon sighed heavily, and David heard the self-recrimination. ''Things I should have seen.''

''Simon...''

''Jeter tripped himself up. He got impatient, cocky. He pushed for your dismissal. A dismissal that was to be fatal. In his zeal, he said some things. Things he shouldn't know. Suddenly, Helen's grandmother wasn't a senile old woman. Everything she'd said made sense.

''Helen wanted to shine. To get ahead. She used Jeter to create a situation. He'd been approached by some comic-opera colonel, had a little information, precious little, that he traded. When she saw her blunder, it was too late.''

''Simon.''

''Let me finish, dammit!'' He wheeled his chair closer to David. ''I should have seen it long before I did. The number you found...''

''Could've meant anything.''

"The bastard had to spell it out for me. I thought he only wanted me. Instead, he betrayed the country, as well. I underestimated him. Worthless files aside, when I added two and two and finally arrived at four, he was already there, with a gun, to silence me. You were next. He'd traced Raven's call and seen her with you at Helen's memorial service. It was that easy for him.

"Perhaps I'm as flawed as Helen was." From the confinement of his wheelchair, Simon looked tired. Illness etched his face, aging what had once seemed an ageless man. "My error almost cost you your life."

"You can't know when every slime takes it into his head to slide over the line, Simon. There aren't enough hours in a lifetime to watch them all. Jeter was a lone wolf hidden in the pack and just obvious enough in his underhandedness to avoid suspicion of more serious involvement.

"As for Helen, she was a damned good agent until infatuation and hunger for glory blinded her. *She* almost cost me my life, not you. Then she gave it back to me. If there's a debt to be paid, she paid hers. Now it's Jeter's turn."

"It will be a long time before he sees the light of day. If ever." Simon's tone altered, softened. "That's it, then? You've come to terms with what happened?"

"I've put it into perspective."

"And your damnable conscience?"

"When a man comes to terms with his conscience, is he still a man?"

"Not a man like David Canfield." Simon offered his hand. When David took it, he covered it with his left. "Good luck, David. Have a good life. When you get to the valley, kiss Raven for me and tell her that I'll thank her in person in a few weeks."

"Then you know."

"That The Watch has truly lost you? Yeah, I know. But who would choose The Watch when a woman like Raven is waiting for him."

"Is she? I brought a lot of pain to her life. There were times when I was worse than a bastard."

"But you love her. I saw that for myself at the games. And she loves you, David."

"She did. A lot has happened that could've changed that."

"Not Raven."

"I haven't heard from her, not in weeks, Simon."

"She had her own grief to work through. Robbie, and then finding Kate."

"Both taken out by a scope shot." David's voice was flat, bitter. "Only Robbie took a while to die."

"It was ugly, David, but she won't fold. She's made of stronger stuff than that. This has been rough on you, too. Raven wouldn't want to pressure you. She's giving you space to decide, to choose."

"I don't need space. I know what I want. I want Raven and a life in the valley."

"Then why are you standing here with me, David? Go to her."

"We both know there will be times when I'll be difficult to live with. No one can wave a magic wand and make my years in The Watch disappear. Is it fair to ask her to struggle with it?"

"The choice is Raven's. Let her make it."

"Yeah." David smiled wryly. "Dean Madison offered me a job. Can you see me as a college professor?"

"I can see you as anything, David Canfield."

"If I have Raven." He realized he still held Simon's hand. He squeezed it, surprised at the returning strength he felt. Someday, when Simon was ready to listen, David would tell him how much he'd meant to him. He'd remind this rough, kind man that he'd saved his sanity—and his life. And with his warning, the life that mattered. Raven's life. David would tell him. Not yet, but soon. "Be well, my friend, and wish me luck."

When David was in the open doorway, framed by its dark wood, Simon called after him, "You don't need luck."

"We'll see."

Simon chuckled. "Were you ever this afraid when you faced the bad guys?"

"I've never been this afraid in my life." David smiled a rueful, lopsided smile and, with a salute, began the long walk down the polished hospital corridor. The echo of Simon's chuckle and then his laughter followed him into the morning.

Raven leaned her head against a piling of the dock, listening to the quiet. The afternoon sun was warm on her face.

Indian summer, a time she loved, the mild, clear days that came like a gift in autumn. A time she was most at peace with herself, her world. But no more. She was restless, unsettled, and had been for days. The valley with its deep dark nights and its flaming days hadn't appeased her.

She had risen this day in a fever, dressed, redressed and dressed again. Nothing felt right. Her skin ached. A futile hour spent at her potter's table produced nothing, achieved nothing. Her gaze had strayed too often with her thoughts to a telephone that did not ring.

How was Simon? Was he well? Were his friends about him? Was David?

David.

Always David.

Her heart had pounded in her throat like a drum. The air in the cabin stifled. The strictures of her clothing became unbearable. She'd found herself dressing again, her hand going to the poet's shirt. David's favorite. The soft fabric had drifted over her bare body like a cloud. Lace caressed and revealed—but there was no one to see.

The path to the lake had drawn her. Shimmering water whispered a silent invitation. She had thought she would swim, remembered David's quiet worry when she did. Instead, she'd drowsed the afternoon away, sitting on the dock, one foot trailing in the cool water, one curled beneath her on the weathered wood.

She missed Robbie and Kate, but in the long, silent weeks, the keen edge of grief had mellowed. She would have other dogs. Someday.

A footstep whispered on the dock and was still. She couldn't turn, couldn't breathe. A breeze teased gleaming curls that escaped from the loose coil pinned at the crown of her head. They tumbled about her throat and shoulders and the swell of her breasts. Fallen leaves of scarlet danced over the dock, rustling and murmuring enticing secrets, leading Raven's gaze to David.

Not the David she'd known, but the man who had first come to the valley, distant, troubled, handsome in his own way. He wore dark, close-fitting trousers with shallow pleats. Token obeisance to current fashion that mattered not one whit to him. His shirt was turquoise, a deep, rich color captured in luxurious silk. The comfortable elegance of the wise and seasoned traveler—the sophisticated mantle of his world. In the glinting sun, a new dusting of silver at his temples hinted of that world's tribulations.

Handsome, distinguished, forbidding. David, but a stranger. An untouchable stranger.

Raven drew a long, anguished breath and looked away from his fathomless eyes. The sound of his footsteps began again, the tap of leather heels, a slow, measured pace bringing David relentlessly nearer.

She meant to rise, meeting him on common ground, and no matter the hurt, keeping her pride intact. Before she could move, he was there, feet planted implacably, waiting for her.

Raven lifted her head, her eyes traveling the length of him deliberately, seeing at close range what she hadn't seen from afar. She was shocked by the man beneath the veneer of elegance. He was handsome, yes, always to her, and distinguished. But not forbidding. He was not an untouchable stranger. He was a man with his heart in his eyes.

His gaze never left her face as he leaned to her and, with a familiar, courtly gesture, offered his hand. Water lapped at her toes, a cricket chirped in a nearby shrub, the shrill cry of a hawk rose over the valley floor—sounds of the valley magnified by its silence and unheard.

Slowly, with a soaring heart, Raven lifted her hand to his. Palms met, fingers clung. Sun-warmed flesh held fast. Then he was drawing her up and to him, spinning with her in the sunlight. Holding her as if he would never let her go. Kissing her. Muttering low, sweet words. Kissing her again. "I was afraid."

"That I would swim alone?" She wanted to hear what she had seen in his eyes. The words. The truth.

He drew the pins from her hair; his hand burrowed in the spill of black gossamer. His voice was husky, rough. The admission of fear, the truth, was not easy for him. "I was afraid you wouldn't want me."

She touched his face, then because she couldn't bear the anguish there, she laid her cheek on his shoulder. "I want you, David," she murmured into the pulsing heat of his throat. "I'll always want you."

He drew a long, slow breath, his chest shuddering with it. His hand slid down her body, holding her to him as if she were fragile, easing the ache of his lonely weeks away from her. When he could trust his voice, he said, "It won't be easy. I'll be difficult, moody, though I won't mean to be."

"Because the memories won't just stop," Raven murmured. "Because in all your years in The Watch, you've never been able to feel that the face of the enemy is the same, whether man, woman or child. Wicked or kind. Vigorous or infirm."

"My weakness."

She stepped away, able to meet his gaze, needing to. "Not your weakness, David. Your strength."

"I came to the valley to find a place of peace, but you became my peace and my strength. I love you, Raven." Her eyes were shining, the look in them enough to bring the strongest man to his knees. She was beautiful. She had never been so beautiful, and it was for him. Yet he felt incomplete. A look was not enough. Dear God! Not nearly enough. "Tell me."

Raven went utterly still. Shock turned her tawny skin pale and her eyes darker than night. She spun about, turning her back on him, moving away. At the dock's edge, she rested one hand on the piling, the other at her breasts. Her back was straight and proud, but her head was bowed.

He wanted to go to her and take her back into his arms. The valley was home now, and none of their differences mattered. This proud, brave woman was his love, the love he would've died for. Only one thing mattered. "Tell me." His voice was raw and aching with his need for the words he'd thought he never wanted to hear. Need became hunger and hunger, desperation. Control that had spun to a fine, thin thread finally snapped. "Dear God! Raven, tell me."

When she turned, her head lifted. Tears glittered on her cheeks. "I love you, David." A smile so lovely, it nearly destroyed him barely curved her lips. "I love you."

She was his sunlight, his hope. When she smiled at him through her tears, he knew she was more than his love. She was his life.

"Raven." His hands were white-knuckled fists. He wanted her. He wanted her with him always. He wanted to spend his life hearing that soft whisper, basking in her love. But had he misunderstood? Was it too late? Had he done too much? Was the danger of loving him unbearable? Her tears, so lovely, so rare... He had to know. Was love enough?

He was hurting. He was desperate. But most of all, he was more than afraid. The chameleon, the proud, lonely man of The Watch was terrified. She was his life. Had he lost her?

A tear trembled on a lash and tumbled down her cheek. With a fingertip, he caught the crystalline drop. It held his world. "Raven?"

If her smile was lovely, her quiet serenity was breathtaking. Her lips brushed his skin where her tear had lain. "I never expected to be so happy. I never thought you'd need to hear that I love you."

David shivered, his body swaying. This was how it was to love. It was pain. It was enchantment. And tears could be joy. His voice was rough and tender. "Simon didn't tell me it would be like this."

"No."

"I think he knew."

"Yes."

"Our oldest sons, Simon first? Or should it be Colin?"

"Simon, I think, and then Colin. After that, I'd like a David."

David laughed. It was a beautiful sound. "In that case, my love, we'd better begin." As quickly as it had come, his laughter faded. "Oh, God! Sweetheart. I thought—"

"Shh." Raven's hand was on his shoulder, and when he opened his arms, she stepped into them. "You couldn't lose me. You never will."

His fingers twined in her hair, binding her to him. His body convulsed against hers. He wanted the words. He wanted to hear her say that she loved him. He knew that he would, over and over again, now that she knew he needed them.

The quietude of the mountains surrounded them as they embraced in the sun.

Raven didn't know how long he held her. He needed her; he loved her. Only that was significant.

When he moved away, his arms still linked about her, his eyes were dark, glittering gold. "Before we begin our little Scots, shouldn't we attend to a little thing called marriage?"

"Later, love." She rose on tiptoe to kiss him. The poet's shirt slid temptingly from her shoulders. "Much later."

His marauding gaze was a caress, his voice a whisper as he drew her slowly nearer. "But not too much later. I don't think it would be wise."

"No." Raven chuckled delightedly at her wonderful, proper renegade and let her shirt of cotton and lace drift from her body.

"David," she whispered when he was only a step away, "I love you."

*   *   *   *   *

NORA ROBERTS

Love has a language all its own, and for centuries, flowers have symbolized love's finest expression. Discover the language of flowers—and love—in this romantic collection of 48 favorite books by bestselling author Nora Roberts.

Starting in February, two titles will be available each month at your favorite retail outlet.

In February, look for:

Irish Thoroughbred, **Volume #1**
The Law Is A Lady, **Volume #2**

In March, look for:

Irish Rose, **Volume #3**
Storm Warning, **Volume #4**

Collect all 48 titles and become fluent in

THE LANGUAGE of LOVE

Ⓢ *Silhouette* ®

LOL292

YOU'VE ASKED FOR IT, YOU'VE GOT IT!
MAN OF THE MONTH: 1992

ONLY FROM

SILHOUETTE® *Desire*™

You just couldn't get enough of them, those sexy men from Silhouette Desire—twelve sinfully sexy, delightfully devilish heroes. Some will make you sweat, some will make you sigh... but every long, lean one of them will have you swooning. So here they are, men we couldn't resist bringing to you for one more year....

A KNIGHT IN TARNISHED ARMOR
by Ann Major in January

THE BLACK SHEEP
by Laura Leone in February

THE CASE OF THE MESMERIZING BOSS
by Diana Palmer in March

DREAM MENDER
by Sheryl Woods in April

WHERE THERE IS LOVE
by Annette Broadrick in May

BEST MAN FOR THE JOB
by Dixie Browning in June

Don't let these men get away! *Man of the Month*, only in Silhouette Desire.

Take 4 bestselling love stories FREE

Plus get a FREE surprise gift!

Coming in February from

SILHOUETTE *Desire*™

MAN OF THE MONTH

THE BLACK SHEEP
by Laura Leone

Man of the Month Roe Hunter
wanted nothing to do with
free-spirited Gingie Potter.

Yet beneath her funky fashions
was a woman's heart—and body—
he couldn't ignore.

You met Gingie in
Silhouette Desire #507
A WILDER NAME
also by Laura Leone
Now she's back.

From the popular author of the bestselling title
DUNCAN'S BRIDE (Intimate Moments #349)
comes the

LINDA HOWARD

COLLECTION

Two exquisite collector's editions that contain four of
Linda Howard's early passionate love stories. To add
these special volumes to your own library, be sure
to look for:

VOLUME ONE: *Midnight Rainbow*
                  Diamond Bay
                  (Available in March)

VOLUME TWO: *Heartbreaker*
                  White Lies
                  (Available in April)

 *Silhouette Books*®